EMMA'S WORLD
Colorado in 1867

The print shop

The Raven

*L
of*

*Frei
offi*

Tildy Pearce's farm

Abbotts' farm

Boardinghouse

WHISTLER
IN THE DARK

❧

by
Kathleen Ernst

American Girl®

Visit our Web site at **americangirl.com**

Printed in the United States of America.
02 03 04 05 06 07 RRD 10 9 8 7 6 5 4 3 2 1

History Mysteries® and American Girl®
are registered trademarks of Pleasant Company.

PERMISSIONS & PICTURE CREDITS
The following individuals and organizations have generously given
permission to reprint illustrations contained in "A Peek into the Past":
p. 157—photograph of Lucy J. Russell, courtesy of Deborah Fontana Cooney;
pp. 158–159—fashion plate, Dover Publications, Inc.; *The Sibyl* masthead, Wisconsin
Historical Society, WHi (X3) 53831; farm woman, Wisconsin Historical Society, WHi (X3) 37029;
pp. 160–161—Sanitary Fair poster and tickets, Wichita State University Libraries, Dept. of
Special Collections, MS 92-25, Kantor Collection; Colorado main street, Denver Public Library,
Western History Dept., X-966; newspaper tent office, National Archives, College Park, MD,
NWDNS-57-HS-718; pp. 162–163—map, Library of Congress; type pieces, courtesy of
Silver Buckle Press, University of Wisconsin–Madison; interior of print shop, Colorado
Historical Society, Denver; homesteader, California Historical Society/Title
Insurance & Trust Co. (L.A.), Collection of Historical Photographs.

Cover and Map Illustrations: Jean-Paul Tibbles
Line Art: Greg Dearth

Library of Congress Cataloging-in-Publication Data

Ernst, Kathleen, 1959–
Whistler in the dark / by Kathleen Ernst. — 1st ed.
p. cm. — (History mysteries)
"American girl."
Summary: In 1867, twelve-year-old Emma and her widowed mother
move to a tiny mining town in Colorado Territory to start a newspaper,
but someone is determined to scare them away.

ISBN 1-58485-486-3 — ISBN 1-58485-485-5 (pbk.)
[1. Newspaper publishing—Fiction. 2. Frontier and pioneer life—Colorado—Fiction.
3. Sex role—Fiction. 4. Mothers and daughters—Fiction. 5. Colorado—Fiction.
6. Mystery and detective stories.]
I. Title. II. Series.
PZ7.E7315 Wh 2001   [Fic]—dc21   2001036635

To Barbara Ernst and Michael MacGeorge

TABLE OF CONTENTS

CHAPTER I
A BAD OMEN

"Mother!" Emma called. Holding her painting carefully, she used one hip to shut the front door behind her. Madame Duchene's praise rang in her ears: "For a girl not yet thirteen, Miss Henderson, you show remarkable promise." Emma could hardly wait to show Mother her latest work.

"You're home!" Mother's voice drifted down the stairs. "Wait in the parlor. I have *two* surprises for you!"

Emma put her package aside. Crackers! What had Mother so excited? The tiny parlor, cluttered with a tea table and horsehair-upholstered chairs and piles of books and magazines, gave no hint. She had sounded . . . happy, that was it. Emma couldn't remember the last time she'd heard that lilt in Mother's voice. Surely not since Father had been killed two years ago, during the final weeks of the Civil War.

Footsteps creaked on the stairs. "Ready?" called Mother. Then she stepped into the parlor.

Emma sucked in her breath. Mother wore a new dress she'd made from brown plaid cotton. She was a good seamstress, and the dress fit well through the bodice and shoulders. But the skirt stopped at her knees. Emerging beneath the skirt, made of the same fabric, were trousers.

Trousers. Loose-fitting, ankle-length trousers.

Mother turned in a slow circle. "What do you think?"

"Mother!" Emma darted to the front window and pulled the lacy curtains closed. "Someone might see you!"

Mother's smile faded. "I'm aware of that." She folded her arms. "Gracious, Emma! I've been a member of the Dress Reform Association for several years. It's about time I had a Reform Dress of my own."

Emma remembered seeing her mother read a newspaper called *The Sibyl,* published by a woman who believed that women's fashions symbolized unfair restrictions placed upon them. And she remembered her mother talking about the need for women to be admired for their talents instead of their fashionable, confining clothes. But she also remembered the only time she'd ever seen a woman in public wearing a Reform Dress—or bloomer costume, as some people called it.

Emma and her best friend, Judith Littleton, had been walking home from art class and saw several boys trailing behind a woman in a Reform Dress as she walked briskly down Harkins Street. "Bloomers, bloomers," they chanted. One snatched an egg from an old man's market basket and threw it—*splot*—against the woman's shoulder. No one had scolded the boys.

The woman ignored them and, with her head high, quickly disappeared around the corner. But Emma was embarrassed for her. "I'm afraid she brought that upon herself," Mrs. Littleton had sighed when Emma and Judith told her about the incident. "It's scandalous. I'll never understand women who wear that ridiculous Reform Dress. Masculine, every one of them. No decent woman would be seen in such a getup."

Emma's cheeks had burned as she hoped desperately that Mrs. Littleton, who had been so kind and loving when Emma's own mother was busy with charity work, would never know that copies of *The Sibyl* were tucked into the magazine rack at the Hendersons' house. Just as her cheeks burned now. Almost every man and woman in America thought the Reform Dress shocking. She had hoped that her mother would never go beyond reading about dress reform.

"Well?" Mother's chin was up, her shoulders back.

"Mother, *please* don't wear that outside." The words slid from Emma's mouth as she plopped into a chair. Her skin felt skittery. She'd never complained when Mother spent more time away doing war relief work than home with her only child. But this! This was too much.

Two spots of color appeared on Mother's cheeks. A flash of anger glinted in her eyes. Then she sighed, and the starch left her posture. She perched on the edge of the low velvet chair in the corner and crossed her ankles, studying the effect. A May breeze ruffled the curtains. Somewhere down the street a dog barked, making Emma painfully aware of the awkward silence in the parlor. But she simply couldn't twist her tongue around an apology.

Finally Mother looked at Emma. "I should have known that this would be difficult for you," she said quietly. "But, Emma, I'm doing this for you as well as for me. I want you to grow up in a nation that respects women's abilities. As long as women are hampered by tight corsets and enormous skirts, we won't be anything more than—than ornaments."

Emma didn't want to be an ornament . . . did she? She wasn't quite sure what that meant. But she did know that she'd die of pure and absolute mortification if her friends ever saw her mother wearing a Reform Dress.

"Women are capable people, Emma," Mother said stoutly. "We *proved* that during the war. Farm women drove reapers and butchered hogs. Women here in Chicago helped keep the factories running while the men were off fighting. We raised thousands of dollars to provide supplies for the army. Why should we be forced backward now that the war's over?"

Emma shrugged, feeling sadness anchor in her heart. The horrible *war* caused this! As if her father getting

killed wasn't enough! Father had left the newspaper he
published to serve as captain of a company in one of the
Illinois regiments that clattered off in the train cars to
war. That was in 1863, when Emma was only eight. For
two long years she and Mother had waited, reading newspaper stories of terrible battles, almost collapsing with
relief each time *The Chicago Tribune* published a list of
killed soldiers without Father's name on it. But Father
had been wounded in some of the very last fighting, and
he died.

Emma looked at the daguerreotype of her father that
sat on the parlor table. Her father's gaze, captured on the
small piece of glass, seemed to take in the room. Whatever
would Father think of Mother's Reform Dress?

Mother stood and walked back and forth across the
room. "It's marvelously freeing," she murmured. "Emma,
I think you'd like it. It just takes some getting used to.
I think I shall make you a Reform Dress, too —"

"I don't want one! What will people think?" Panic
began to bubble in Emma's chest. Even if she didn't wear
the Reform Dress, Mother was obviously determined to.
Great glory, what would Judith say? Would Mrs. Littleton
tell Judith not to spend time with Emma anymore? Would
the pastor preach against the Hendersons from the pulpit?
Would boys throw eggs at *her,* just for being Mother's
daughter? The skin between her shoulder blades tingled,
as if the egg had already hit. *Splot.*

"I'm not interested in what other people think," Mother snapped. "I want you to develop your own thoughts and opinions. What do you want from life?"

Emma squirmed. What she most emphatically did *not* want was a mother wearing a Reform Dress, with its short skirt and horrid trousers. Not when all of her friends pinned fashion plates of floor-swishing silk dinner dresses from *Godey's Ladies' Book* to their bedroom walls. Not when all of her friends' mothers—even those who had done war work—were settled back into their former lives, content to be wives and mothers and wear hoop skirts that brushed the tops of their shoes.

"You're old enough to consider these things," Mother said finally. "At your age, I was already earning my keep in the newspaper office. And I was already finding doors closed, just because I was female. I had hoped you'd support my efforts to change that now. But I won't force you."

Good, Emma thought. She struggled to find something to say to break the uncomfortable silence. Suddenly she remembered. "Didn't you say you had *two* surprises?"

Mother's eyes began to sparkle again as she picked up an envelope from the table. "This arrived today. Emma, it's finally happened! I've been offered a position as newspaper editor!"

Emma's stomach flip-flopped as her mother slid the letter from the envelope. Oh, no. *Oh, no . . .*

When the first tide of grief had passed after Father's death, Mother had driven Emma to distraction with talk of making a new start. Mother had answered dozens of advertisements from small towns all over the West, where, she hoped, people might be more "open-minded." Most of her letters had gone unanswered, although a few town representatives wrote to advise her that their job was not open to a woman. As the months passed, Emma had put the whole notion out of her mind. "Where?" she whispered.

"A town called Twin Pines. It's in Colorado Territory."

Twin Pines, Colorado Territory. A strange, wild place far from Chicago. Emma sagged back in her chair.

Mother leaned toward the window and began to read:

Dear Mrs. Henderson:

I have reviewed your long letter and am pleased to offer to you the position of newspaper publisher and editor. Twin Pines is a growing town in the foothills of the Rocky Mountains. It is a service center for the farmers and ranchers in the area, and a staging spot for miners heading up to the goldfields. I humbly introduce myself as town founder. You will be pleased to know that town lots for a church and a school were among the first to be set aside. I designed the business district to grow around a proper town square, with residential neighbor-hoods beyond. I noted your request for a house on a lot large enough to accommodate a garden, and will provide a print shop rent-free for your printing press. If you are still interested in the position, please commence the trip with all possible speed, for Twin Pines desperately needs a newspaper. I am enclosing the particulars regarding travel arrangements. You may respond with your intentions to this address.

Your most obedient servant,
James M. Spaulding

Please commence the trip with all possible speed. Emma clenched her hands into fists. "But I don't want to move to Colorado Territory! It's—it's a wilderness!"

"It's not a wilderness. Twin Pines sounds like a nice little town." Mother sighed. "Sweetheart, I know it will be a big change. But we've talked about this before! You knew I was looking for a position somewhere in the West."

I didn't think you'd find one, Emma wanted to shout. She pleated her skirt between her fingers, avoiding Mother's gaze.

Mother's voice grew thin. "Emma, try to understand. I . . . I need to make a new beginning. Here in Chicago, I'll never be anyone but Mrs. Richard Henderson."

And why was that so terrible? Emma fought back tears, missing her father so much that she could hardly breathe. Their little house that leaked around the windows during

heavy rains, and never heated properly, and barely held
the half-dozen ladies wearing huge hoop skirts who had
gathered every Thursday during the war to sew shirts for
the soldiers—why, it had never seemed so dear.

And what about *her*? Would she have good neighbors
in Colorado? The kind who brought custardy *blanc mange*
when Emma felt poorly, as Mrs. Beecher had? Would
Emma find a friend like Judith Littleton? Judith had
been Emma's dearest friend ever since, as five-year-olds,
they had been assigned to share a desk on their first day
of school. These people, this neighborhood, Chicago—
this was home.

Why were Mother's causes always more important
than Emma? Mrs. Littleton's scorn rang in her memory:
"Scandalous . . . ridiculous . . . masculine . . ." Mrs. Littleton
had done war work too, but now she spent her afternoons
embroidering monograms on handkerchiefs and teaching
Judith and Emma how to tat lace. Only Emma's mother
wanted to move to the wild frontier and march through
life wearing a Reform Dress, with no regard for her
daughter's feelings.

Emma stared at the floor. If they stayed in Chicago,
she would be shamed beyond words by her mother's
Reform Dress. The only escape was moving to horrible
Colorado Territory. She was trapped. It wasn't fair! But
as Emma opened her mouth to protest, her father's very
last words to her rang through the years: "Be a good,

obedient girl for your mother, Emma. She'll need your help. Promise?" Emma had promised. Surely Father hadn't known that Mother would announce a wild plan like this! Still . . . Emma had promised.

"I think Twin Pines will give us new opportunities," Mother continued. "I'm looking forward to writing articles. Most will be news, of course, but I hope I can make a difference by letting Colorado women know about the reform movement. And I'm counting on your help with the newspaper. Perhaps you can write a special column for young people."

Composition was Emma's least favorite subject in school. *"Mother—"*

Before Emma could continue, Mother gasped and jerked to her feet. All hint of color drained from her cheeks.

For an instant Emma thought that her lack of enthusiasm had caused Mother such distress. Then, through the open window, Emma caught a snatch of a whistled tune fading into the distance. *Maggie by My Side.*

The hair on the back of Emma's neck prickled, and goosebumps rose on her skin. "Father used to whistle that tune. Just like that."

"Yes," Mother managed. *"Exactly* like that."

Emma shivered. "Maybe it was Father's ghost—"

"Don't be ridiculous." But Mother's voice shook—just as it had the day the letter about Father's death arrived.

She picked up the daguerreotype and drew a deep breath, staring at the image. "It was your father's favorite song," she said in a faraway tone. "My parents always called me Margaret, but your father called me Maggie. I haven't heard a man whistle *Maggie by My Side* since your father enlisted in the army."

Emma flew to the window. Twilight shadowed the street. She heard the clip-clop of a team of horses pulling a carriage down the muddy street, and the Beecher boys whooping over a croquet game next door. Nothing more.

"I imagine it was just a worker heading home." Mother pressed the daguerreotype against her heart before replacing it on the table. "We were silly to let it startle us so."

Emma stared at the carpet. She didn't think they'd been silly. The whistled tune echoed in her head, and another shiver scuttled over Emma's skin. Father had been dead for two years. And now they heard his special song, whistled just as Father used to, on the very evening Mother tried on her first Reform Dress? Just as she announced plans to take Emma from their old family home and move to the wilds of Colorado?

If it wasn't Father's ghost, it was an omen. A bad one.

CHAPTER 2

COLD WELCOME

Silas banged the stagecoach door open and grinned at his two passengers. "Here we are, ladies!"

Emma took a deep breath. *Here we are.*

After two weeks of frantic packing, she and Mother had spent endless days rattling west in train cars and, finally, a stagecoach. In eastern Colorado Territory, the lush green of prairies had given way to an arid, sandy brown, sprinkled with prickly pear cactus and tufts of silver sage. This morning, the road had left the flat plains and climbed along what felt like a boulder-strewn path. Now, she and Mother had finally arrived in their new home.

Emma's mouth felt dry. Silas offered his hand to Mother before helping Emma step down to the ground.

Twin Pines was situated along a creek in a long, high meadow. Emma's gaze went first to the rocky hills rising sharply beyond the town. The nearer slopes were marked only with stumps, but pine trees dotted the higher elevations. Emma couldn't remember a bluer sky.

Suddenly, several sharp explosions shattered the afternoon. "Good gracious!" Mother gasped, grabbing Emma's arm. "Was that gunfire?"

"Nothing to fret about!" Silas spat a stream of tobacco juice into the street, aiming away from their skirts. "Somebody's just letting folks know the mail's in."

The stage had stopped in the middle of what appeared to be Twin Pines' single street, and people were already hurrying toward the coach. Silas tossed a leather pouch toward a short, balding man wearing a once-white shirt and limp cravat. The short man stepped up on a mounting block and began pulling envelopes from the mailbag. "Jack Tomkins! Nels Torkelson! Nathaniel Russert! Hang on, there, it's still ten cents a letter!"

Emma's heart sank. Why, she could almost throw a rock from one end of town to the other! Twin Pines boasted fewer than a dozen frame buildings. Some of them, square and proper, were labeled with signs: *General Store, Boardinghouse, Land Office,* and *Hardware and Mining Supplies.* A line of horses stamped at the picket pole in front of the largest building in town—a saloon.

The rest of the town faded down the street with a curious, rickety air. Some buildings had been constructed of rough logs. A number of businessmen apparently worked from canvas tents. A collection of odd cabins and shacks sprawled haphazardly on the rolling ground around the town. The street itself was a washboard of ruts and mud, and Emma knew why the men tucked their trousers into their boots. An unfortunate combination of rotting potato parings and ox droppings scented the afternoon.

Dismay settled on Emma's shoulders. Twin Pines looked nothing like the tidy village Mr. Spaulding had described.

He had lied, Emma realized. Thunderation! He had lied!

"Excuse me, is this really Twin Pines?" Mother asked Silas slowly.

"Yes, ma'am." Silas shifted his attention to his assistant, who had clambered to the top of the coach, where supplies and the Hendersons' carpetbags had been lashed down. "Start with the ladies' luggage, Bob."

Mother frowned. "But Mr. Spaulding's letter said . . ."

"Did Spaulding paint a pretty picture?" Silas shook his head. "That's a land speculator for you. He's a promoter. Staked every penny he's got on this town, so I hear. Came out from New York and bought lots of land cheap, so he could sell it to farmers and businessmen as prices rise. Spaulding's desperate to bring new immigrants out from back east."

"Mother—" Emma began, but she saw fire in Mother's eyes and swallowed the accusation she wanted to shout: Look what you've done!

The driver caught one of their carpetbags and set it

off to the side. "I'll be here long enough to rest my horses and get a meal, ma'am. Let me know if you want me to load your luggage again and take you back."

Emma caught her breath. Oh! *Could* they go back to Chicago?

"Leave it there for the moment," Mother said in a clipped tone. She looked around grimly. "I expected to be met," she muttered. "Emma, wait for me here." She marched toward the Land Office. Emma was glad Mother had decided to travel in a sensible gray dress instead of the horrid Reform Dress. She looked formidable enough as it was.

Silas set the other carpetbag at Emma's feet. "This is yours too, ain't it?" Emma nodded miserably. Silas was chewing tobacco, and he wore a huge bowie knife on his belt and smelled of sweat and onions—and he was the most familiar thing in sight! Tears threatened, and Emma blinked hard.

"There's some good folks in town," Silas said, as if reading her thoughts. "Oh, say, did that fellow find you and your mother last night?"

"What fellow?"

"Never saw him before. He stopped in the stable and asked if Mrs. Henderson and her daughter were on my stagecoach. I told him you were inside the station house. Didn't he find you?"

"No." Emma frowned. "What did he look like?"

"Well, it was dark, and I was tending a horse with a loose shoe, so I didn't get a good look. Short fellow. Had a limp, I think. Smelled like he'd been traveling hard."

Emma crushed a clod of dried mud beneath the toe of one boot, considering. She'd heard someone whistle *Maggie by My Side* again last night as she was dropping off to sleep. "You must have been dreaming," Mother had said crisply this morning—just as she had when Emma had thought she'd heard the tune again in Chicago. But Emma *knew* she hadn't been dreaming. Was Father somehow trying to reach his widow and daughter? Fear and hope mingled in a quick shiver before she shook her head. Father had stood taller than most men, and a ghost wasn't likely to ask a stage driver for directions—

"Emma?" Mother called, hurrying forward with a portly man in tow. "This is Mr. Spaulding."

"How do you do," Emma said reluctantly, sizing up the man who had painted such a rosy picture of this miserable town.

"I trust your trip went well?" Mr. Spaulding asked. The buttons on his maroon paisley vest looked ready to pop. Beneath a dusty top hat, his forehead glistened with sweat, although the afternoon smelled like rain and a cool breeze made Emma appreciate the sun sifting through her shawl. He pulled a handkerchief from his pocket and dabbed at his forehead.

"The trip was uneventful." Mother's voice was hard.

"But, Mr. Spaulding, I must be frank. My first glimpse of Twin Pines does not reveal the idyllic town you described in your letters."

"Oh. Yes. Well, I—ahem—I have occasionally been accused of describing the town as I know it can *become,* instead of as it is. I'm sure you'll forgive me that indulgence." Mr. Spaulding didn't quite meet Mother's eye.

"Is there a church?"

"No. That is—not yet. Although Miss Holly has organized Sunday gatherings. Bible readings and hymn singing and such."

Mother pursed her lips. "What about a school? I expect Emma to attend a proper school in the fall."

"And she will! That's what, three months away? I'm sure . . . that is, by then . . . with a little luck . . ." Mr. Spaulding's voice trailed away as he reached for his pocket watch. "Not quite one o'clock!" he concluded, as if that had direct bearing on the conversation. "Silas made good time."

The man was impossible. This place was impossible! No church, no school—why, it was horrible!

Mother glanced at the luggage, then at Silas, who was heading toward the saloon. "I'd like to see our house, sir," she said. "And then the newspaper office."

"Yes! Yes, of course. The freight driver delivered your equipment two days ago. As to your accommodations . . . ahem! I'm afraid I've had to arrange for temporary quarters. Right this way." He picked up their two carpetbags and led the way—to a two-story frame building labeled "Boardinghouse."

Emma's spirits, already low, dipped further. A boarding-house!

"You did promise us a house of our own." Mother's tone could have sliced lard.

Mr. Spaulding nodded vigorously. "Yes, yes, of course. I—ahem!—am already working on that small detail. There are shortages, you understand . . ."

Emma gave Mother a pointed glance. What kind of people stayed at such places in squalid little towns like Twin Pines? What accommodations were provided for bathing and . . . other necessary things?

Mother stared at the boardinghouse, looking unhappy. But after a moment she pinched her lips again and followed Mr. Spaulding up the steps.

Mrs. Sloane met them with a broom in hand. A stout woman, she wore a faded blue dress and a no-nonsense air. She briskly swept some fine dirt into a pile, then set the broom aside and extended her hand. "You must be the Hendersons. Pleased to make your acquaintance."

Mr. Spaulding waited in a small sitting room while Mrs. Sloane gave Emma and Mother a tour. "Dining room's in through there." She indicated a closed door. "Breakfast is served between seven and eight. Dinner at noon, but I can wrap you a cold meal to take if you prefer. Supper at six."

Mrs. Sloane led Emma and Mother up the stairs to a scrubbed but cheerless room overlooking the street, furnished with two beds, a dresser, and a desk. Their trunks, sent ahead by freight wagon, waited. Mother's sewing machine sat in one corner—ready to sew more of the horrid Reform Dresses! Emma turned away.

"Thank you, Mrs. Sloane," Mother nodded. "We'll settle in later."

As Mr. Spaulding led them back outside, a boy about Emma's age darted up. "Hello! Are you the editor-lady?"

Mother smiled. "Yes. I'm Mrs. Henderson, and this is my daughter, Emma."

"Well, we've been waiting ever so long for a news-paper!" The boy revealed a gap-toothed grin. He tipped his faded felt hat and then planted it firmly back on his black curls. "I'm Jeremy Abbott. My pa's still rounding up the mail, but he'll want to meet you."

"Jeremy's father was one of the first settlers to buy land from me. He's got a farm north of town," Mr. Spaulding said as they set off, with Jeremy trailing along.

Jeremy's welcoming smile couldn't dispel the distaste gnawing at Emma as they walked through town. What would Judith make of this raw place? Of the sudden burst of song from the saloon as they passed, or the chicken bones and rags tossed into the street? Of the line of men's underwear flapping from a clothesline near a laundress's tent? Of the mule train and freight wagons, with their

curse-spewing drivers cracking long black whips? Of
the brave false fronts on the saloon and store, as if the
buildings—just like Mr. Spaulding—needed to pretend
things were more important than they were?

Just then a single rider turned into the main street
from a side alley. A young brunette woman rode sidesaddle on a small bay horse. She wore gloves and a trim
straw hat, and a peach-colored dress that spread like an
open flower against the horse's dark coat. *She could be
from a Godey's fashion plate,* Emma thought, mesmerized
by the unexpected sight of a vision from the pages of her
favorite magazine.

The woman smiled. "Welcome to Twin Pines!" she
called. Emma managed a sincere smile in return.

"Howdy, Miss Amaretta!" Jeremy called, adding to
Emma, "That's Amaretta Holly."

Ah—the Sunday school lady. Emma gazed after
Miss Amaretta Holly. Even her name was lovely.

Mr. Spaulding led them down the boardwalk fronting
the little row of frame buildings. Emma heard her mother's
sharp intake of breath as they stepped back down into
the muck and kept going. "I don't see any telegraph lines,"
Mother observed suddenly.

"We hope to get lines sometime this year ... or perhaps
next year."

"But—how am I to get news? People will want news
from the East."

"Denver City has telegraph service. That's only twenty miles or so away. I'm . . . working on arrangements," Mr. Spaulding said vaguely. He tramped past several cabins and finally stopped in front of a large canvas tent. "Here we are."

"Mr. Spaulding!" Mother stopped. "I assumed we'd have a roof over our heads!"

Mr. Spaulding nodded. "And you will! In time. I did get your equipment unpacked, you'll be pleased to see." He held one of the canvas flaps aside invitingly.

Emma ducked inside first, dodging a lantern that hung from the ridgepole. The tent was larger than their parlor back home in Chicago, but crowded with rough-hewn tables lining the two side walls. The printing cabinet holding trays of lead type stood in one corner. The printing equipment—galley trays, type sticks, and the heavy dismantled gear of her father's old Washington Hand Press— had been spread neatly across the tables.

And a single piece of paper, hand-printed with large letters, lay in plain sight:

NO JOB FOR A LADY!

Emma caught her breath. Mr. Spaulding, following her mother into the tent, paused for only a second before smoothly scooping up the paper, crumpling it in his fist, and sliding it into his pocket. "As I said, I did unpack your equipment for you," he said, as if the note had never existed.

Even in the dim light, Emma saw Mother's cheeks flush. "Evidently someone in this town doesn't approve of your choice of editor, Mr. Spaulding."

"A joke, I'm sure, nothing more," he muttered. "If you only knew how people had hounded me to hire an editor and get a newspaper established—*hounded* me! I assure you, all that most people in this town want to see is a good weekly paper. We have a floating population of about one hundred."

"And more farmers and ranchers outside of town," Jeremy added. "And lots of men passing through, headed up to the mining camps. Everybody'll want to subscribe. There's nothing else to read."

Mother drew a deep breath and folded her arms, looking over the equipment. "Who have you hired to work with me? I'll want to get the press assembled as soon as possible."

Mr. Spaulding cleared his throat. "I have not quite been able to finish those arrangements. You understand, it wasn't practical to hire anyone until you arrived! Men need steady employment, and so many are just passing through . . ." His voice trailed away.

The stuffy tent got very quiet. *Things are even worse than I imagined,* Emma thought. But she felt so sorry for her mother, and so embarrassed for Mr. Spaulding, that she spoke up. "We can't run the paper alone, sir." Mother flashed her a look of grateful surprise.

"I'll help!" Jeremy offered.

"That's very kind, Jeremy," Mother said, then swung her gaze back to Mr. Spaulding. "Let me understand. You've brought me and my daughter all the way from Chicago to start a newspaper, and you have no office for me to work from. No pressman. No typesetter. No printer's devil. No telegraph station. And someone in this town is already offended that you hired a woman for the job."

Mr. Spaulding's forehead beaded with sweat, and he pulled out his damp handkerchief again. "That seems to be the case, Mrs. Henderson," he admitted. "And the truth is, I wouldn't blame you and Emma if you decided to get back on that stagecoach and go home. Wouldn't blame you one bit."

Emma and her mother locked gazes. *This is all a horrible mistake!* Emma wanted to shriek. *Let's go home!* But she saw in Mother's eyes a tiny bit of foolish, stubborn hope. Emma remembered how happy Mr. Spaulding's invitation had made Mother. And she remembered her own promise to Father, that she'd be obedient. Reluctantly, Emma tried to keep any pleading from her face as she waited for Mother's decision. A man brayed with laughter somewhere nearby. A heavy-loaded wagon rumbled past the tent.

"No, sir," Mother said finally. "I'm not ready to give up before I even begin." Jeremy beamed. Emma let out the breath she was holding, torn between disappointment and pride. Her mother was many things, but she wasn't a quitter.

While Mother and Mr. Spaulding discussed business details, Emma looked at the disassembled press. She ran a finger over the wooden tympan, which held sheets of paper during the printing process, and the iron forestay, which supported the bed holding the type. She knew every aspect of the press almost as well as her mother did. Precious memories of Father's newspaper office rose again now: the astonishing speed of the typesetters' fingers, the smell of cigar smoke and ink, the printers' grunts as they labored over the creaking equipment, the sense of urgency as Father and his small staff rushed to make deadline.

Father hadn't wanted Mother to work in the press shop after they got married, but sometimes Mother had helped out in a pinch. Emma recalled watching her mother set the type, letter by letter, for Father's stories. When the war began, Emma sometimes helped Father at the shop while Mother organized Sanitary Fairs and other events to raise money for the soldiers. After Father enlisted, Mother tried to juggle the newspaper and her relief work, but when the foreman quit, Mother decided to cease publishing the newspaper altogether. Emma remembered feeling a mighty loneliness as she looked at her father's printing press, standing silent and still.

But here in this strange new place, the disassembled press didn't seem sad. Here in Twin Pines, Colorado, was wood and iron that Father's hands had known. Emma smiled as she touched each piece, visualizing the press being reassembled, brought back to life—

She stopped abruptly, daydreams gone, and took another mental inventory. Then she looked under the tables and in the empty packing crates. "Mother," Emma cried, "the press lever is missing!" During the printing process, the iron lever was pulled to force the paper against the inked type.

Mother quickly took her own inventory, then turned on Mr. Spaulding. "Emma's right! It's missing!"

"But . . ." He spread his hands, looking confused. "Everything was laid out when the crates were unpacked yesterday. Are you sure it was packed?"

"Quite sure! I supervised the packing myself, back in Chicago."

"Then . . ."

"It seems that leaving my equipment alone overnight in a tent wasn't a wise decision, Mr. Spaulding," Mother snapped. "I can't operate a printing press without a lever!"

Emma heard the high, brittle note in her mother's voice, and saw that her hands were clenched into fists. Was Mother feeling the same chilly shiver that whispered down Emma's neck? Someone in Twin Pines didn't want them there.

CHAPTER 3

CHOICES MADE

That's done it, Emma thought. *This will surely push us back to Chicago.* She opened her mouth to suggest that they go catch Silas before he left—then shut it again. A slow steam of anger was burning away that painful ball of loneliness and unease in her chest. She hated Mother's decision to bring them to this awful place. But even more, she hated seeing Mother so shaken. How dare some—some *stranger*—treat them this way?

Emma stood straighter. "We can fix it," she said.

Mother shook her head. "We can't fix something that's been stolen."

"Surely we can rig something up!"

Mr. Spaulding looked doubtful. "We're a long way from any source of new equipment for a printing press."

"How about wood?" Emma asked. "Maybe someone could carve us a new lever."

"I bet my pa could do it!" Jeremy offered. "He can carve anything."

"We'd need a very strong wood," Mother said slowly. "Pine wouldn't do."

Jeremy grinned. "Mountain mahogany. It's strong as iron, almost. Pa can—"

"What's this you're promising me for?" A stocky man with hair as black as Jeremy's walked into the tent.

Jeremy introduced Mother and Emma and explained about the missing lever.

"Pleased to meet you, ma'am, miss." Jeremy's father doffed a sweat-stained felt hat. "I'm sorry to hear there's been mischief. My boy's right, though. Mountain mahogany'll do the trick. Tell us what you need, and we'll get you fixed up."

"Oh, thank you." Mother's words emerged in a flood of relief. "I can make you a sketch, with measurements. But—I still must have a room I can lock so that this doesn't happen again."

Mr. Abbott turned to Mr. Spaulding. "How about that place where Gus Stevens sold mining supplies?"

"Is it empty?" Mr. Spaulding blinked, looking confused.

"Gus cleared out three days ago. Got gold fever himself, I heard. It's off the main street, but it'll do."

Mr. Spaulding nodded. "I own that lot. That will do nicely. I'll pick up a new padlock at the store."

But Mr. Abbott was still frowning. "Mrs. Henderson,

I got to ask you one thing plain. This town needs a newspaper real bad. Running a business is ten times harder out here than back east. Are you up to the job?"

"Yes, Mr. Abbott. I am." Mother's voice was firm.

But Mr. Abbott wasn't convinced. "I invested every penny I had in my farm, and me and my boys have put two years of sweat and labor into making it a go. Lots of other folks around here have staked everything they've got on this place, too. Twin Pines is set up prime to serve the farmers and ranchers hereabouts, and the miners heading up into the hills. But this town is going to die if we don't attract new settlers and businessmen from back east. And to do that, we need a good newspaper. Nobody around here can afford to see the newspaper fail because you're here on a fancy."

Emma drew in a long breath. *Almost* nobody, for someone had already tried to dishearten her and Mother. Still, she hadn't realized how much was riding on the success of the newspaper.

But surprisingly, Mother smiled. "Mr. Abbott, I have no intention of letting this paper fail."

"I appreciate that, ma'am, but do you know how to—"

"I started working as a typesetter when I was Emma's age. During the four years I spent at that, I learned everything there is to know about the mechanical needs of a printing press. Then I married the publisher's son. My husband became publisher a year later when his father died, and he taught me a great deal about the business. After my husband enlisted in the Union army, I oversaw the newspaper's operation for another six months. I ceased publication only because I wanted to devote my energies to war relief work. I was very active in the Sanitary Commission—which, as I'm sure you're aware, saved countless lives by raising money to provide healthy food and medical supplies for soldiers in need."

Emma dared a glance at the two men. Both were listening intently.

"In addition, I served on the steering committee of the 1863 Chicago Sanitary Fair," Mother went on. "I negotiated contracts, oversaw construction of the exhibition pavilions, and managed fund-raising activities that ultimately raised more than one hundred thousand dollars to help our soldiers. I am quite capable of conducting business outside of the home."

Mr. Spaulding blinked. Mr. Abbott's eyebrows raised.

Mother was still building steam. "I'm here to make a success of this newspaper. And I have a very capable daughter to help me. I don't pretend for a moment that it will be easy. We have subscriptions to solicit, advertisements to sell, news to gather. We have stories to write and set, paper and ink to secure, and a small staff to hire. All this, knowing that someone in this town already wants Emma and me to fail. But I assure you, gentlemen, that it will be done."

That torrent of assurance left Mr. Spaulding speech-
less. Mr. Abbott nodded, looking pleased. A reluctant
smile tugged at the corners of Emma's mouth. Whoever
wanted her and Mother to pack up and leave town was
going to be very disappointed.

☙

Homesickness balled in Emma's throat that evening as
she unpacked the few mementos she'd been able to bring
from Chicago. She put her copy of Father's daguerreotype
on her half of the dresser and placed her precious packet
of letters from him beside it. She put a little shell-covered
box that Judith had given her beside the letters. The box
held a mourning brooch made with a lock of Father's hair.
She propped up one of her paintings and pinned a fashion
plate from *Godey's* on the wall. Only then did she feel ready
to slip into her own nightgown and slide between the
sheets. They smelled of lye soap.

Mother was silent as she put on her nightgown and
brushed her hair, then opened one window a bit to let
some cool mountain air into the stuffy room. She got
out her notebook and pencil, but she only stared at the
blank page.

Emma finally broke the silence. "Who do you think
could have left that note and stolen the lever? I can't imagine who would be willing to sacrifice having a newspaper,

and all the good it can do, just because the editor is a woman. Who would be so mean?"

Mother rubbed at a flyspeck on her notebook. "I have to believe it's just a mischief-maker—someone who thought it would be funny to see if a woman editor would have the vapors at the first sign of trouble."

Emma didn't think it was the least bit funny. Did he have more tricks in mind?

Mother sighed. "Oh, Emma. Twin Pines is not at all what I expected."

"Maybe you shouldn't have taken Mr. Spaulding's word for everything," Emma murmured. It was disrespectful, but honestly! Mother prided herself on her business sense!

"You're right. I didn't ask enough questions. After all the rejections, I was just happy to get Mr. Spaulding's letter. I guess I wanted to believe that everything would work out."

Emma stared at the ceiling. She didn't know what to say.

Mother turned down the oil lamp, and darkness cloaked the room. Several moments passed before she spoke again. "I'm quite unhappy with Mr. Spaulding for misleading us."

Emma was too, but she thought she understood his deception. "He needs you, Mother. It sounds like a lot of people around here need you."

"They need us, Emma. I couldn't do this without you,

you know. You kept your wits about you this afternoon, just when I was at wit's end. I was very proud of you."

The unexpected praise made Emma feel guilty for her lukewarm support of this newspaper venture. She was still thinking that over as she heard Mother's breathing deepen into the rhythm of sleep. She wished she could talk to Judith—

Suddenly Emma sat bolt upright in bed. Through the open window came the faint but unmistakable sound of whistling.

Someone was whistling *Maggie by My Side* . . . with the same jaunty style, the same pause on the high note, that she'd heard from Father a thousand times before he went to war. Just as she'd heard the tune whistled again in Chicago as she and Mother prepared for the journey west, and again on the road. *Exactly* the same.

Emma clutched the quilt to her chest as a shiver whisked down her spine. "Father?" she whispered, wishing she could claw away the darkness. Her heart hammered.

The last whistled note, held long, seemed to hang in the night air. Then—nothing, except Mother's even breathing and faint shouts from the saloon across the street.

Emma finally lay back down. But a long time passed before she stopped trembling and fell asleep.

CHAPTER 4

MEETING THE BOARDERS

The next morning, Emma woke to the noise of male voices and heavy footsteps in the corridor—the other boarders. She kept her eyes closed, remembering the threatening note and the stolen press lever, the whistled tune and the icy ball of fear she'd felt, wondering if Father's ghost was near. Emma wished she could stay in bed. Should she tell Mother she'd heard *Maggie by My Side* again? Surely she could convince Mother that she hadn't imagined it—

"Good morning, Emma." Mother's cheery voice punctured Emma's thoughts. Her spirits lifted as she splashed some water into the bowl on her nightstand and washed her face. The aroma of frying bacon beckoned beneath the door. Sunlight streamed through Mrs. Sloane's starched muslin curtains. The last shreds of Emma's fear faded. If Father . . . well, if his *spirit* could come back, he wouldn't want to frighten her! The whistler was surely a real man.

Maggie by My Side had been a popular tune. Probably every man in Colorado knew it.

"Well, Emma? Do you want to wear your Reform Dress today?"

Emma looked up from the towel. Mother had insisted on making her one of the horrid trouser costumes. It hung now from a peg on the wall, cranberry red with white spots. "Mother, I told you I wouldn't!"

"I had hoped you might change your mind," Mother said quietly. "I thought it would be a fitting way to start our new venture together. But it's your choice. That's what dress reformers want to do—encourage women to make their own choices."

Emma hesitated. "Mother, maybe you should wait a day or two. What if . . . what if Mr. Spaulding isn't comfortable having a dress reformer in charge of his town newspaper?"

Mother raised one eyebrow. "I mentioned my interest in dress reform in my introductory letter. It didn't stop him from hiring me."

Crackers. Emma tried to think of a new argument. "But someone in this town is already unhappy because Mr. Spaulding hired a woman. Maybe—"

"*Emma.* I've already said I'd accept your decision. Now I'm asking you to accept mine."

I can't, Emma thought, remembering the thrown egg, and Mrs. Littleton's scorn, back in Chicago . . . and Mrs. Sloane's proper air . . . and how beautiful Miss Amaretta

Holly had looked riding sidesaddle, her skirt draped and flowing. *I simply can't.*

Emma dressed slowly, hoping Mother would go downstairs without her. She chose her good wheat-colored dress with braid trim and took special care arranging her hair. Perhaps if *she* dressed well, people would be less judgmental about Mother's attire. She studied herself in the mirror. Perhaps the mourning brooch would help as well—

"Emma Catherine Henderson!" Mother stood by the door. "I—am—waiting."

"I'm coming!" Emma said, but she couldn't help adding, "Mother, aren't you at all afraid of what people will say? What if—what if someone throws an egg at you?"

Mother lifted her chin. "I believe in what this costume stands for. My husband went to war because of something he believed in. How can I be afraid of a few taunts, or even an egg or two? Come along, now."

Emma followed Mother down the stairs, wrestling with guilt and embarrassment. Through the open dining-room door she could hear a cheerful babble of voices—

Which fell utterly silent as Mother walked into the room.

As Emma followed, she saw Mrs. Sloane, standing rigid with a steaming coffeepot in one hand. She saw astonishment on the faces of the two men seated at the table . . . *and* on the face of Miss Amaretta Holly.

Miss Amaretta boarded here, too? Emma considered

pretending that she'd never met her mother before and only chance had brought them into the dining room together.

The silence became painful before Mother found her voice. "Good morning!" she chirped. "I'm Mrs. Henderson, and this is my daughter, Emma."

Miss Amaretta studied her plate. Emma's cheeks flamed. She wished she could melt into the floorboards.

"Why . . . good morning!" One of the men, a handsome blond of middling age, jumped up to pull out a chair. Then he paused, as if unsure whether a woman in Reform Dress would accept his gesture. With a gallant smile he stepped back, indicating the chair with a flourish: a successful compromise. "You must be the newspaper editor we've heard so much about."

Emma slid into the empty chair beside Mother's. Mrs. Sloane collected herself and silently poured coffee for the Hendersons. Emma sipped the scalding, bitter stuff, grateful to have something to do.

The man reseated himself. "Call me Blackjack," he said, looking mildly amused. He was dressed impressively in a pair of checkered wool trousers with a dark coat, brocade vest, and striped cravat.

"That's an unusual name," Mother said, reaching for a platter of chipped beef. Her cheeks were flushed. Emma suddenly realized that this first public appearance in Reform Dress was more challenging for Mother than she wanted to admit.

The second man had followed the exchange with a sour look. Unlike Blackjack, he wore the worn trousers, wool vest, and stained work shirt of the miners Emma had seen in the street. "'Aces' would be a better name," he observed in a humorless drawl. "He's usually got an extra up his sleeve."

"I own The Raven—the saloon across the street," Blackjack told Emma and Mother calmly. He used his knife blade to sprinkle salt on his fried potatoes. "I'm afraid my good friend Dixie John here has lost a poker game or two at my establishment."

Dixie John. Emma sucked in a slow breath. This man was Southern! Had he been a Confederate soldier? Had he fought against Father?

Dixie John scowled. "I don't mind losing in a fair game," he muttered, then addressed Mother. "What will our newspaper editor have to say about a crooked gambling house?"

"I don't write stories based on hearsay," Mother said carefully. "But if I find firm evidence of illegal activity, I will write the truth."

Mrs. Sloane emerged from the kitchen and set a basket of biscuits on the table. "Mind your tongue," she warned Dixie John. "I'll have no trouble stirred up under my roof." She marched back into the kitchen.

"I ain't aiming to stir up trouble. Just asking a few questions of the editor-lady here." Dixie John leaned back in his chair. His gaze swung from Mother to Emma. "I'm trying to decide if I should subscribe to the paper or not," he continued, looking back at Mother. "I may not be inclined toward your politics. I may not be comfortable with your family background, so to speak."

Emma couldn't bear his wordplay for another moment. "My father was a captain in the Union army," she said with cold pride. "Is that what you wanted to know?" So there!

Mother squeezed Emma's hand beneath the table. "My daughter and I are proud of my husband's service," she told Dixie John quietly. "But the war is over."

Dixie John shoved away from the table. His boots clattered down the hall. The front door slammed. He began to sing as he stumped down the steps, and the words drifted through the window: "Oh, I wish I was in the land of cotton, old times there are not forgotten, look away, look away, look away, Dixie Land . . ."

Emma balled her napkin in her lap and willed the wave of hate within her to subside. Hate wouldn't bring back Father.

Blackjack dabbed at the corners of his mouth with his napkin. "Well said, Madam Editor. But one wonders. There is not much news worth reporting in this dusty hole."

"I must disagree," Mother said evenly. "We've been here less than a day, and several stories have already presented themselves."

"I'm delighted to hear it. I'd hate to think you would have to dig too far to find material. That could be most . . .

challenging, for ladies in your situation." Blackjack's smile
included them both, but Emma didn't feel reassured. Was
Blackjack concerned about their welfare? Or was he hiding some kind of threat behind his polished words and
fancy clothes?

Mother met his smile with one of her own. "You'll be
relieved to know that my daughter and I are up to the
challenge. Every journalist knows how to dig for a story.
It's usually a simple matter of asking the right questions—
who, what, why."

"Mrs. Henderson, I see you have matters well in hand."
Blackjack stood. "Good day, ladies." He nodded at Mother,
Emma, and Miss Amaretta in turn before ambling out of
the dining room.

Mother pressed her lips together for a moment, then
said briskly, "Emma, are you finished? We need to get
started as well."

"Mrs. Henderson." Miss Amaretta Holly leaned forward. "A moment of your time, if you will."

"Why, certainly." Mother settled back in her chair.

Miss Holly flushed a delicate pink. "I must ask . . .
do you truly intend to wear that—that dreadful *costume*—
about town?"

Thunderation. Between Dixie John and Blackjack,
Emma had almost forgotten the blasted Reform Dress.

"Most certainly," Mother said coolly.

"I wish you would reconsider."

Mother raised her eyebrows. "I beg your pardon?"

Emma's cheeks flamed. *Mother, please don't argue with Miss Amaretta,* she pleaded silently.

"Let me tell you a little story." Miss Amaretta drew a deep breath. "Over a year ago, my brother left our home in Ohio and traveled west to try his luck at gold mining. When he stopped writing, I came looking for him. Our parents were already dead, you see. We just had each other."

Emma stared at her lap. Surely this story didn't have a happy ending.

"I traced him here, to Twin Pines, and learned that he had been shot and killed during a brawl in The Raven." Miss Amaretta's voice trembled a bit, but she firmed it up. "I came very close to heading back to Ohio. But I saw too many other young men getting into trouble—drinking, gambling, heading up to the hills to pan for gold instead of tending to families. I decided to help build a decent community here, so that no other sister or mother would suffer a loss as I did. Men like Dixie John, boys like my brother, even Blackjack . . . they need a good, *womanly* influence. I've started a small dressmaking business, but much more importantly, I've started holding Sunday school. And I'm organizing a musical evening, with the proceeds to go toward a reading room or school—"

"I'll be happy to promote your efforts in the newspaper!" Mother's smile worried Emma.

Miss Amaretta flushed again. "But Mrs. Henderson . . .

I'm afraid that you wearing that costume will undermine my efforts. Creating a strong, *decent* sense of community is very important to me."

Miss Amaretta might as well have tossed a lighted firecracker onto the table! "Then we all have a great deal in common," Emma said brightly. "Mother and I believe a good newspaper will help build that sense of community." She stood up. "Mother, are you ready to go?"

Mother waited until they were outside before speaking. "Emma, that was very diplomatically said." She paused. "But it's important for me to discuss dress reform with people like Miss Holly."

"She seems nice," Emma mumbled as they started toward the print shop. She ducked her head when she noticed several people stop and stare.

"Yes, she does. And I respect her beliefs. All I ask is that she respect mine as well."

Remembering the look on Miss Amaretta Holly's face when she saw Mother's Reform Dress, Emma doubted that that would ever happen.

❦

Emma began her first workday by sorting type. Mother had brought three sizes, called fonts: small for news articles and advertisements, larger for article headlines, largest for the newspaper title and major headlines. The hundreds of tiny lead pieces, each bearing the imprint of a single letter or punctuation mark, had become jumbled during the trip. Emma sat before the typecases—open wooden boxes with small compartments designated for each letter—and began organizing the type. The job was tedious, but important. Whoever set type for Mother's articles would need to know exactly where to reach for each letter.

Mother began her first workday by arguing with Mr. Spaulding. He garnered some favor by only nodding at Mother's attire, murmuring "How practical." But Mother had no intention of compromising her needs. "Mr. Spaulding, you *promised* me two helpers." Mother's hands were planted on her hips, and the look on her face almost made Emma feel sorry for Mr. Spaulding. "I can't accept anything less. Emma and I have turned our lives inside out based on your hollow promises. We need to get this equipment moved to the new print shop. I need a strong man to manage the press, and—"

"I, um . . . I expected that finding suitable help would be an easy undertaking. There are always men in Twin Pines looking for work—miners whose claims didn't pan out, or farmers' sons looking for a few extra pinches of gold dust. But I didn't quite account for the—the opposition to, well, that is . . ."

Emma paused, watching Mr. Spaulding shift his weight miserably from one foot to the other. He was already sweating, even though the morning was still cool.

"Mrs. Henderson, no one is willing to work for a woman."

Mother's eyes narrowed. "I see."

Impatience surged through Emma. How stupid!
She was starting to understand why Mother wanted to
encourage what she called "social reform."

"I will continue to look for the help you need,"
Mr. Spaulding assured them. "And in the meantime,
I am willing to offer my services, such as they are."

Mother looked doubtful. Emma considered Mr.
Spaulding's thick fingers. His hands looked as if they'd
never done more than lift a pen. A "haloo" from outside
the tent broke the awkward silence. A moment later
Mr. Abbott ducked inside, followed by Jeremy and an
older, taller boy.

They stopped cold when they saw Mother's outfit.
"Great guns!" Jeremy exclaimed.

"Hush," his father said, then turned back to Mother
with a composed air. "Good morning." He waved a
rough-hewn piece of wood vaguely resembling a press
lever. "I started this last night on my shaving bench, but
I wanted to check the fit before finishing it off. And this
is my oldest boy, Clark. I thought you might need a hand
moving your equipment. We can spare a morning away
from the farm."

"Mr. Abbott, *bless* you," Mother said. "Your arrival
couldn't be more timely."

"I'm delighted—delighted!" Mr. Spaulding pumped

Mr. Abbott's hand. "And I have other business to attend to." He disappeared with rather astonishing speed.

Jeremy's father leaned against one of the worktables, shaking his head. "When I bought my land from Spaulding, he was sure Twin Pines would thrive. He was full of enthusiasm! Now I think he's given up. He even offered to buy my place back. I think he feels guilty. A lot of us believed his promises of a boomtown."

Mother frowned. "He can't have given up completely. He did bring me out here to start a newspaper."

"When do you think you'll have a paper ready to distribute?"

"Well, my plan is to start with a prospectus—a single printed sheet, letting local people know that we're here and looking for subscribers and advertisers. If all goes well, I should have the prospectus ready in a few days. Then we'll work on the first real issue. I want a standard four-page newspaper, with one page for national news from the East, one page for local news, one page for notices and editorials, and one for literature and items of family interest. Emma will help with that."

"Here's the situation." Mr. Abbott dropped his voice. "My brother is visiting from back home in Indiana. He says about twenty families there are considering emigrating west. They're splitting off from their congregation and want to settle together. And they haven't chosen a final destination yet. Mrs. Henderson, I want them to choose Twin Pines. If they come here, we'll soon have a church. One of the men is a schoolteacher. And that many families could buy up most of the land Mr. Spaulding's still sitting on, so he'd get back his investment and have the capital he needs to invest in further improvements."

"That sounds lovely!" Mother's face glowed.

"My brother has to leave for Indiana on the next stagecoach. That's six days from today. If he waits any longer, he'll miss the meeting where those folks decide where to settle. I want him to take fifty copies of your four-page newspaper with him. A good newspaper will give them a sign that we're a settled, stable community. Mrs. Henderson, can you get that paper done in time?"

Emma bit her lip, thinking that through. Six days! That didn't give them much time, especially if whoever didn't want them there had any more mischief in mind. But thinking about that steamed Emma up all over again.

"Absolutely," Mother announced, just as Emma said, "Yes, we can." They exchanged a startled glance. Then Mother flashed Emma a huge grin.

Mr. Abbott nodded, satisfied. "Emma, Mrs. Henderson," he said, "it's going to be a pleasure doing business with you."

CHAPTER 5
UP IN FLAMES

With the deadline agreed on, the Abbotts manhandled the press equipment into their wagon and transported it to the new print shop on the outskirts of town. The one-room shack had been constructed from broken-down packing crates. Words like *NAILS* and *LAMPBLACK,* faded but still visible, marched sideways or even upside down on some of the boards. The floor was sawdust. But two real windows provided light, and the door could be locked.

Emma spent the morning organizing the typecases while the others assembled the heavy printing press. "Oh, that's wonderful!" Mother exclaimed, when the Washington Press was ready. "I don't know what to do next—start composing articles, or head out to let people know that we're ready to take advertisements and subscriptions."

"Why don't you let Jeremy and me do that?" Emma

suggested. Her eyes were about to cross from squinting at the tiny letters. Besides, if Mother stayed in the print shop, fewer people would see her wearing trousers. And while Emma talked with townspeople about the newspaper, she could listen for suspicious remarks that might signal the troublemaker. "Jeremy can introduce me to people."

After munching a cold lunch of beef and biscuits, Emma and Jeremy set out. Emma used one hand to keep her hem from trailing in the eggshells, cabbage leaves, and gnawed bones littering the street. In the other hand, she carried a small notebook, a pencil, and an old issue of the paper her mother had published in Chicago.

"Remember," Mother called after her. "Write down one piece of news about each person." Emma nodded.

Jeremy led her first toward a cabin labeled *Freight Office,* which fronted a scattering of buildings near the creek. Emma hesitated. She'd seen plenty of freight haulers on the road—both muleskinners, who rode the rearmost mule of a string pulling a wagon, and bullwhackers, who drove a team of oxen from the high seat in their big wagons. Most cursed like blazes, and they all cracked whips above the backs of their animals with nerve-plucking regularity. Rough men, all of them.

Could one of *them* have left the note and stolen the press handle?

Emma eyed the leaning shack proudly labeled *Warehouse.*

Near it was a stable, a small corral, and a fleet of heavy wagons and draft animals. "Let's go," she said. She followed Jeremy into the tiny freight office.

"Mr. Torkelson!" Jeremy greeted a wiry, ragged blond man behind the counter. "This is Emma Henderson. She has some business to discuss."

"Hello, Emma!" Mr. Torkelson said. "What iss it I can do for you?"

Emma's tongue suddenly froze. She couldn't conduct business with men—especially men with thick accents and tobacco-juice stains on their stubbled chins. It wasn't proper! Why hadn't she let Mother plunge out to face the town herself?

Jeremy frowned, tipping his head toward Mr. Torkelson.

Emma swallowed hard. "Well, sir, I'm ... that is ... well, you probably wouldn't want to subscribe to a newspaper, would you?"

Jeremy rolled his eyes, and Emma felt her cheeks burn. *You'll never sell a newspaper like that,* she scolded herself. But honestly! English was obviously Mr. Torkelson's second language, and he needed a bath a great deal more than a newspaper.

But Mr. Torkelson nodded. "Oh, ya! Mr. Spaulding told me you were coming."

"Here's an example of my mother's work." Emma spread the old newspaper carefully on the plank that Mr. Torkelson used for a counter. "*The Twin Pines Herald* will be a weekly." Her voice was still skinny, and she tried to flesh it out. "It will have both national and local news."

"How much will it cost?"

"Annual subscriptions, paid in advance, are four dollars. Advertising space is four dollars for six lines for six months." She opened her notebook and waited with pencil poised.

He grinned. "Ya, sure, I'll subscribe."

"You *will?*" Emma released her breath in a whoosh. "Oh, thank you! I'll write your name down. You can stop by the print shop and pay my mother."

"Don't got time for that. I'll give you gold dust up front."

Crackers! Her mother hadn't said anything about taking gold dust.

"That's fine," Jeremy said, nudging her—hard—in the ribs.

Emma's eyes widened as Mr. Torkelson pulled a small leather pouch from his pocket and poured a trickle of gold granules onto a small scale. Some were tiny as grains of sand, some bigger. Squinting, Mr. Torkelson added small round brass weights to the other side of the scale. After removing a pinch of gold dust, so that the scale was balanced, he scooped the tiny pile onto a piece of paper, folded it up, twisted the ends, and handed it to Emma. "Here."

Emma tucked the twist into her pocket. "Thank you!" Her first sale—paid in gold dust! She wanted to whoop. Then she remembered the rest of her assignment. "Oh, yes—is there anything new in the freight business?"

Mr. Torkelson rummaged in his pocket and brought out a pouch of tobacco as he considered. "Well, one of my boys iss bringing in a load of goods this afternoon—the store-keep ordered three new bolts of calico for the store. The ladies might like that, ya? Ah! And I almost forget. The paper shipment iss due this afternoon, too. Mr. Spaulding ordered it for you ladies. I'll have it hauled to the print shop when it arrives."

Emma nodded, scribbling. "Wonderful. Thank you again." She shook his grimy hand before she and Jeremy headed back outside.

"Our first subscription!" Emma said happily. Was this how Mother felt when she accomplished something new?

"You did pretty good," Jeremy allowed. "Once you got started."

"But I needed your help about the payment."

"Your mother will need to get a scale. Most folks around here pay up with gold dust. Nuggets are scarcer—they're worth a lot of money."

Emma and Jeremy found more enthusiasm as they made their rounds. The barber, who worked from his wagon, subscribed. So did the hard-muscled woman who took in laundry. The blacksmith and the livery-stable

owner both wanted to advertise their businesses in the
newspaper. No one acted unfriendly or suspicious.

"Let's stop by Mr. Spaulding's office," Emma said as
they neared the center of town. "I want to tell him how
well we've been doing."

A rock propped open the land-office door. Emma
paused in the doorway, admiring Mr. Spaulding's large,
ornate desk and several gleaming chairs upholstered in
black horsehair. A table held a row of ledgers, and several
large maps hung on the back wall. An oil lamp with a fancy
base adorned one corner of the desk, a brass coatrack and
matching umbrella stand stood near the door, and a square
carpet graced the floor.

But Mr. Spaulding, at the desk, sat over an open ledger
with his head in his hands. Emma could just make out
neat columns of figures marching down the ledger page.
Suddenly he muttered an oath and snapped the book shut.

Emma rapped on the door frame. "Mr. Spaulding?"

His head jerked up. "What? Oh—come in."

"We just wanted to tell you that everybody we've talked
to this afternoon subscribed to the newspaper," Emma said.
"We should have *The Herald* up and running in no time."

He rubbed his temples. "I only hope it's not too late."

Emma glanced at Jeremy. Thunderation! Was Mr.
Spaulding giving up on Twin Pines before she and Mother
even got the newspaper going?

Mr. Spaulding pushed his pen and inkwell away, closed

the ledger, and reached for a large, polished wooden box sitting on the side of his desk. Opening the lid, he slipped the ledger inside on top of a pile of papers. Then he closed the box and snapped a tiny lock in place. The box was made of warm golden wood, with swirls in the grain. It reminded Emma of the box where her father had kept *his* correspondence tools. Father's box had those same unusual swirls in the wood. As a child, Emma had loved to trace them with a tiny finger, and to hide little surprises for Father in the box—a flower, a tea cake she'd brought from home . . .

Emma drew a deep breath, swiping away a tear. Unexpected reminders of Father still punched like a fist. She avoided Jeremy's curious gaze by focusing on one of the maps. Unlike the others, it was encased in a frame carved from walnut and gilded with paint. "Mr. Spaulding? What's that?" Emma pointed.

Mr. Spaulding led them to the map, which showed a small city. Emma had seen similar maps back in Chicago. Prepared by insurance companies, they were called bird's-eye maps because they were drawn from the perspective of a bird approaching overhead. Every building and street was clearly visible.

Mr. Spaulding regarded the map sadly. "This was my vision for Twin Pines."

Emma stared. The Twin Pines of the land speculator's dreams was a bustling town of shops and homes and churches and schools, laid out on a neat grid of clean streets around a pretty town square. The map artist had added carriages and pedestrians, all looking stylish and serene. It was the town Mr. Spaulding had described in his letters.

"Oh my," Emma murmured.

"Oh my, indeed." The land agent shook his head.

"Mr. Spaulding, don't give up yet," Jeremy begged.

"We're picking up lots of subscribers," Emma reminded him. "Oh, and the freight-wagon man said he expects that the paper shipment you ordered will arrive today! We'll soon have our prospectus ready to go."

Jeremy waited until they were outside before letting out a long breath. "Whoo! He sure seemed down."

"Business must really be bad. Maybe he had to borrow money from a bank to buy up all the land around here, and now they want him to pay it back." Emma sighed. "Where to now?"

Jeremy led her toward the general store. "Mr. Boggs will be glad to meet you," he promised.

Inside the store, Emma recognized Mr. Boggs as the short man she'd seen dispensing the mail the day before. He was busy with a woman who was fingering bolts of cloth, so Emma had a chance to look around. The store offered barrels of crackers and cornmeal, piles of gleaming tin basins and lamp chimneys, boxes of buttons and soap, and shovels and buckets—all the basic necessities. But there wasn't much variety. And the prices! Fifty cents for a single pickled egg. A dollar for a peach. Common calico, thirty cents a yard.

"I'll be right with you two," Mr. Boggs called. He pulled pieces of brown paper from a huge roll behind the counter, unwound string from a big ball of twine, and wrapped the woman's goods. "Thank you, Mrs. Barker," he said, and then he turned to Jeremy and Emma. "Who's your new friend here, Jeremy?"

When Jeremy made the introductions, Mr. Boggs beamed. "I'm glad to support the paper. In fact, I'd like to talk with your mother about printing some special broadsides. Notices of sales and new items."

"We can do that," Emma promised. "My mother can tell you what it will cost."

Before they left, Jeremy asked for two peppermint sticks. "My father said it was all right to put it on his account," he said. Once outside, he cocked his head at Emma. "Come on. Let's take a break."

He led Emma down a narrow alley that ran between Mr. Spaulding's land office and the saloon, away from the noise and filth of the main street. They emerged beside a towering pine tree—or was it two pine trees? Emma looked at the twisted trunk and wasn't sure if two trees had grown together, or if one tree had produced two trunks.

Jeremy dropped beneath the overhanging branches. "This here's the twin pines. Mr. Spaulding had his land office built right in front because he thought it was a good landmark. It's one of my favorite spots." Emma hesitated— wearing her best dress hadn't been a bright idea after all—then sat down beside him. He handed her one of the peppermint sticks and grinned. "Here."

"Thank you!"

"Everybody seems happy about the newspaper," Jeremy said between licks of his candy.

"*Somebody's* not happy." Emma gave Jeremy a sideways glance. Surely she could trust him! "My mother wants to believe it was a joke, but I really want to find out who stole the press handle and left that note. All morning, every time we passed someone, I'd think, 'Is it *him?*'"

"I can't figure it."

Emma's stomach curled as she remembered seeing that note. "Do you know a man named Dixie John? He stays at the boardinghouse. He wasn't very nice to me and Mother this morning."

"He's a drifter. Gets gold fever every now and then and heads up to the hills. Comes back every time, either with gold to gamble and drink away at the saloon, or flat busted and looking for work. Ends up digging wells or chopping wood to make ends meet." Jeremy shook his head. "He's an ornery sort. Had a hard time in the war, they say. Never got over the Confederacy losing."

"My father was in the Union army. I wonder if Dixie John could be so bitter about that that he'd try to cause trouble for Mother and me. But . . ." She shook her head. "The press lever got stolen before he'd ever met us!"

Jeremy drew a deep breath and blew it out again, considering. "Well, he might have known your pa was a Union officer. I knew it."

Emma stared at him. "How?"

"Your mother said so in her letter to Mr. Spaulding, and he told my pa." Jeremy swatted a mosquito. "Your mother getting hired was big news."

Emma turned that information over in her mind. "My mother said that a journalist looking to figure out a story asks simple questions—what, who, why. In this case, the 'what' is that someone wants the newspaper to fail." Emma thought for a moment, then pulled out her notebook. She wrote *Who* across the top of one page, and *Why* on the facing page. Underneath she penciled *Dixie John* and *Hates Unionists.*

Trying to sort things through sensibly felt better than just wondering and worrying. "What about Blackjack?" she asked. "Something about him made me nervous, and Dixie John accused him of cheating at cards."

"Well . . . Dixie John might just be mad because he lost a few poker games."

Emma twirled a pine needle between her fingers. "If Blackjack is dishonest, he might not want a reporter in town. He might be afraid that Mother will write an article about the accusations. It would be bad for his business."

"Maybe." Jeremy didn't look convinced.

Emma wrote *Blackjack* and *Something to hide?* in her book. "Can you think of anybody else?"

"Not offhand."

Emma leaned against the tree trunk. It was pleasant to smell pine instead of the manure and garbage in the street. In this quiet moment, she could almost imagine the vision that Mr. Spaulding and Miss Amaretta Holly had for the town . . .

Emma caught her breath. Miss Amaretta hated Mother's Reform Dress, didn't she? And Mother had mentioned her interest in dress reform in her letter of application. "Before we got here, Jeremy, did you hear that my mother is a dress reformer?"

Jeremy wrinkled his forehead. "No. If your mother said so, I don't imagine Mr. Spaulding cared much—if he even knew what a dress reformer was."

Still, Mr. Spaulding might have mentioned Mother's ideas about dress reform to Miss Amaretta. Could Miss Amaretta have stolen the press handle? Ridiculous! Emma couldn't bring herself to even mention that idea to Jeremy. Still, Emma scribbled *Miss A. H.* and *Disapproves of Reform Dress* before slapping her notebook shut.

"Let me know if you think of anyone else who might want to make trouble for us," she said. "It means everything to my mother to make a go of it here."

"To my pa, too."

"I'm starting to figure out just how important the newspaper could be," Emma said slowly. "To help attract a minister and schoolteacher and more farmers, and all."

Jeremy sucked his peppermint stick for a moment, staring at his toes. "It's more than that to my pa," he said finally. "My ma didn't want to come here. They argued about it, back in Indiana, after I was in bed at night. Pa said it would give me and my brothers a better foothold in life, to come out here where land was cheap. She finally gave in, but she up and died on us a few months after we got here."

"I'm really sorry." Emma understood. Did sudden memories still take Jeremy by surprise? Did unexpected reminders bring tears to his eyes—like that beautiful swirly-wood box of Mr. Spaulding's had for her?

"After we buried her, Pa stood over her grave and promised her that our farm would succeed. 'It won't be a waste, Betty,' he told her. And then he bawled like a baby." Jeremy swallowed hard. "Some folks farming up the valley from us have already bailed out. It would break my pa down if our place fails and we have to move on. The day Mr. Spaulding offered to buy Pa out, talking about how sorry he was that Twin Pines hasn't turned out like he planned, and how it looks like the whole place is going to go bust—that was a bad day."

"Well, *The Twin Pines Herald* will attract new settlers. You'll see."

Jeremy smiled. "I think so, too."

Emma crunched the last bit of candy between her teeth. "That peppermint sure tasted good. Thanks again. This is the nicest time I've had since leaving Chicago. What do you do for fun around here?"

"Oh, lots of things. You like to climb trees?"

Emma blinked. "Um, no. That is, I never tried."

"This is a great one." Jeremy patted the twin pines. "Climbs easy as a ladder, and you get an eagle's view once you're up a ways. Once when Clark was pestering me something awful, I slipped away and climbed up. I spent an hour watching him search the whole town for me."

"That's terrible!" Emma protested, but she couldn't help smiling. "I like to paint. Do you like art?"

"Naw. But I collect rocks. A professor once came through, surveying for one of the mine companies, and he taught me a few things."

"Did he find any gold?" Emma asked. "A gold mine around here could solve Twin Pines' troubles!"

Jeremy smiled. "There's gold in the creek, but not so's you could make any money from it. Placer mining—what folks back east call panning for gold—that played out years ago around here. But rock hunting, now that's pretty good. I've found agates and rhodochrosite and some nice quartz. Want to come with me sometime?"

Emma fumbled for words. She didn't want to hurt Jeremy's feelings, but climbing trees and hunting rocks was not her idea of fun! "Well . . . I expect my mother will keep me pretty busy," she managed finally.

If he was offended, he didn't show it. "Do you ride?"

"No." Emma sighed wistfully, remembering how lovely Miss Amaretta Holly had looked on horseback.

"I can teach you. We've still got my mother's sidesaddle." Emma gave him a genuine smile. "I'd like that."

Before heading home for afternoon chores, Jeremy promised to return the next morning. "We can sell more subscriptions," he promised as they walked back to the main street. "We didn't talk to everybody in town, and we have to ride out to the farms and ranches around here."

Emma waved good-bye and turned toward the print shop. Now that so many people were excited about the newspaper, maybe the troublemaker would leave them alone . . .

A man bellowing from down the street interrupted her thoughts. Was the stagecoach coming in? No, Silas wouldn't be back till Monday. A saloon brawl? Or maybe—

"*Fire!*" someone screamed.

Fire! Clutching up her skirt, Emma ran toward the commotion. In a moment Emma saw the crowd gathering at Mr. Torkelson's freight business. Smoke shivered skyward. Emma eeled through the throng. Beside the warehouse shack, a waist-high pile of goods was burning. Flames licked greedily at the shack wall's dry planks.

Mr. Torkelson had already organized a bucket brigade

stretching from the well behind the stable to the fire. "Get the buckets! Ya, ya, there!" A tight feeling squeezed Emma's chest as she watched the men frantically passing buckets.

With amazing speed, the men put out the fire. The shack wall was charred and smoking, the goods beside it were reduced to ashes, and the stink of smoldering wood hung in the air. But Mr. Torkelson's business was intact.

"That was close," breathed a woman standing near her. "Thank God there was no wind. The whole town could have burned to the ground." People jostled around Emma, muttering and shaking their heads.

Emma remembered to pull out her notebook and make a few notes. She should find out how the fire started. Mr. Torkelson was hollering in what she guessed was Norwegian to two younger men, and she edged closer.

Then the freighter saw Emma and strode toward her. "Oh, Miss Emma..."

"Do you know how the fire got started? I'm going to write a story for the newspaper—"

"The newspaper!" Mr. Torkelson snatched his hat and slapped it against his thigh, looking frustrated. "That's the problem, ya? My building iss not so bad hurt. But the paper..."

The paper. Something cold twisted in Emma's belly. "The shipment of paper? The one you told me about? *That's* what burned?"

He nodded. "I am sorry. I never had such trouble in my business before. You can ask anybody—"

"How did the fire start?" she interrupted.

"I don't know. My driver—my son Lars—came in right on time. We unloaded that shipment of paper along with everything else, and I set it off to the side so I wouldn't forget to deliver it straight off. Well, I did have some papers to check first. I got to do that right away when a load comes in. So I go back inside, and Lars goes off to help his brother tend the horses. Suddenly I hear, 'Fire! Fire!' I run outside and see that crate of paper burning." He shook his head again.

"That was our paper that burned," Emma murmured. She felt dazed and sick and angry, all at once. "The shipment we need to print the newspaper on." Good glory. What would she tell Mother?

"I am sorry. And I'll make it right by you, ya? We'll get word to the nearest telegraph office, and they'll get another shipment started. Or maybe we can buy some in Denver City or Golden. I'll work it out with Mr. Spaulding."

"How long will it take to get the new shipment here?"

"At least several days. Maybe more." Mr. Torkelson fingered his suspender straps, looking miserable. "It wass a terrible accident."

Accident, my foot, Emma thought. She didn't believe it for a second.

CHAPTER 6
BREAK-IN

O h, my." Mother sank down on her bed as the evening sun disappeared over the mountains. "Too much is happening."

Emma began unbraiding her hair. "I'd say so." The stolen press handle, the fire—not to mention the whistling, which Mother hadn't even heard here in Twin Pines—it all made her feel cold to the bone.

"I'm ready to start setting type for the prospectus. But we don't have any workers. And now we don't even have paper to print on." Mother sighed. She sounded ready to quit. To go *home*.

"Mother," Emma said quietly, "maybe we should give up."

Mother studied her fingers, then looked at Emma. "It's not that simple. Two train tickets, two stagecoach tickets, paying to get the press and our things freighted out here ... well, it was all very expensive. I still have a bit of money tucked away, but it's not enough to get us back to Chicago."

Emma's hand stilled. *What?* She'd known that Mother didn't *want* to go home, but it felt very different to know that they *couldn't* go home. Is that why Mother wasn't trying to find out who was behind all the trouble? Since she'd made the decisions that had left them stranded in Twin Pines, was it easier to believe the theft a prank and the fire a coincidence?

Mother tried to smile. "Things will work out. But at the moment, I'm too tired to think straight." She stood up and kissed Emma on the top of the head. "You go to bed. I need to visit the outhouse before settling down."

Emma turned out the lamp, slid into bed, and lay staring at a shadow on the ceiling. They were trapped in Twin Pines . . . with someone who didn't want them there. Could Dixie John have started the fire? Maybe she should ask Mr. Torkelson and his sons if they'd seen Dixie John around. She could take her notebook, ask a number of questions—make it sound like she was simply working on a newspaper story—

Whistling pierced the night. *Maggie by My Side.* Emma jerked upright in bed.

For a moment she couldn't move. Goosebumps raised on her skin. In the silence, the jaunty tune sounded somehow eerie and menacing.

As the last note faded away, Emma bounded out of

bed and darted to the window. The night was cloudy, and
she caught only a glimpse of a shadowy figure melting into
the darkness. Was it The Whistler?

Lamps glowed in the windows of The Raven. The
faint scratch of a fiddle drifted across the street. A man
stumbled out the saloon doors. Two more men trotted
up on horseback, tied their mounts, and disappeared inside.
Heart still pounding, Emma jumped when the door
behind her opened.

"Emma?" Mother asked. "What are you doing?"

"Just looking out the window." Emma let the curtain
drop and slid back into bed. A moment later the ropes
supporting Mother's straw mattress creaked as she got
into bed, too.

Emma curled into a tight ball. Who could know
that *Maggie by My Side* had unique meaning for her and
Mother? And . . . could The Whistler be the person trying
so hard to stop them from publishing the newspaper?
Had he followed them all the way from Chicago, asking
Silas about them on the road to be sure he hadn't lost
them? If so, the trouble was suddenly much more
personal—and scary. Emma's skin prickled. "Mother!"

"Yes, dear?"

Only the weariness in Mother's voice stopped Emma
from blurting out her fears about The Whistler. Mother
was already worried. Emma didn't have the heart to add
to her burden tonight.

"Nothing," Emma muttered. Shivering, she inched farther down in bed.

᥷

The next morning, Emma woke feeling as if cobwebs draped her brain. Avoiding Mother's hopeful gaze, she left her Reform Dress on its peg and pulled on her plain work dress.

As she and Mother walked to the print shop, she didn't regret her choice. A few people—folks she'd met the day before—gave them friendly nods as they passed, but others gawked at Mother's costume. One young man pointed and hooted, "Hey, lady! You forgot your skirt!" Emma stared at her shoes, cheeks flaming.

"I shall stay in the office this morning," Mother said as they neared the shop, "in case any subscribers come to make their payment. Will you go ask Mr. Spaulding to stop by? I want to know—" She stopped, staring at the newspaper shack with dismay.

"Mother? What's wrong?" Nothing looked amiss—

Wait! There. The lock that Mother had secured the evening before hung open. Emma's bones went cold.

Mother drew a deep breath, tugged the dangling lock free, and pulled open the door. *Don't!* Emma wanted to cry. *Maybe The Whistler is waiting in there.* But Mother charged inside before Emma could speak.

When she followed, Emma felt a sinking sensation in her stomach. The press cabinet doors were open. The typecases lay on their sides, discarded. And the type—hundreds of tiny bits of lead, which she had spent *hours* sorting and organizing the day before—was scattered over the sawdust floor.

"That's enough." Mother sounded defeated. "That is absolutely the last straw."

Emma dropped to her knees. The different type fonts were jumbled together, some pieces already buried in the sawdust. It would take *forever* to collect and sort the type again. Emma blinked hard as tears of frustration scalded her eyes. This *was* the last straw . . .

Then anger began to steam away her despair. "You're right," she said slowly. "That is enough. Now I am really, *really* angry." She glared at the type as if it had jumped from the cases. "Thunderation! This is just too much!"

Mother stared at her with wide eyes. Suddenly she burst out laughing. Emma didn't see the joke. But she was relieved to see color coming back into Mother's cheeks.

"Oh, I'm sorry," Mother gasped, wiping her eyes. "But you look so fierce, sitting there in sawdust. I wish whoever did this could see you right now."

A knock on the door frame interrupted them. "Excuse me. Miz Henderson?" A big Negro man stood just outside, hat in hand. His skin was black as the best ink. Muscles showed through his thin work shirt.

Mother composed herself. "I'm Mrs. Henderson, and this is Emma. May I help you?"

"I heard tell you might be looking to hire."

"Yes," Mother said. "We are."

"I don't have no experience with a newspaper," the man said quietly. "But I learn quick."

Mother tipped her head, considering. "What is your name?" she asked after a moment.

The man shifted his weight. "Folks call me Mule."

"Mule!" Emma burst out. That was a horrid name!

"Yes, miss. On account of me being strong as a mule." A smile played at his lips. "Them that gave me the name didn't intend a compliment. But I've come to carry it that way."

Watching his face, Emma wondered where Mule had come from, what his life had been like. Had he been a *slave*? She had met a few Negro people in Chicago, but never a former slave. Seeing Mule's eyes, sensing what might lie behind his soft words, Emma felt very young and ignorant.

Mother extended her hand. "Please come in. If you're going to consider working with us, there are a few things you need to know. First, the workdays are likely to be long. I need a strong man to handle the press, but I'll need help with other jobs, too. Can you read?"

"Yes, ma'am."

"Good. Second, someone has decided that Twin Pines doesn't need a newspaper run by a woman." Mother gestured to the mess of type. "We've been having . . . incidents. Someone broke in last night and caused more mischief."

The big man looked around the shop. "I could sleep here, if you like. Ain't nobody likely to get past me."

"Do you live in Twin Pines?" Mother asked.

"I'm just in from Big Gulch. Haven't had much luck prospecting, but I ain't giving up till I earn me enough to buy a good piece of farmland. I need a job so I can fix me up another grubstake and head back to the goldfields."

"If I can't scare up a shipment of newsprint, this job won't last long," Mother said. "By coming to work for us, you're taking what some may see as an unpopular position."

Again, that ghost of a smile. "I figure I've been in that hole before." He didn't seem particularly worried. Emma smiled encouragingly.

"Do you have references?" Mother asked.

"I done some odd jobs last time I passed through town. You could ask at the freight office, or Miz Sloane's place. Can't nobody say my word or my work ain't good."

"Fine. Just one more thing." Mother looked up at him, square in the eye. "I won't call a man 'Mule.'"

His silence grew so long that Emma's nerves began to flutter. She didn't want him to walk away now. The curses and whip-snaps of a teamster prodding his string of oxen down the street drifted into the little shack.

Then the big man nodded. "A long time ago, my mama called me Thomas. 'Mule Tom' might suit."

Mother smiled. "That will do."

Phew! They were back in business.

⌒⌒

Emma left her mother and Mule Tom to work out the details. As she headed down the street, she found herself looking over her shoulder. Was *that* man The Whistler? Or that one, in the red shirt? It felt horrid to know that some stranger was working so hard to frighten her and Mother. Why? *Why?*

She found Mr. Spaulding in his office. "We had more trouble," she reported grimly. "Someone broke into the newspaper office last night. Dumped over the typecase. The lock was hanging open when we got there this morning." Emma plopped into a chair. "Mother wants to know if you kept a spare key to the padlock."

"Why—ahem! Yes, I did. I have keys for most of the buildings that sit on lots I still own. I learned the hard way to do that. Too often men up and leave for the goldfields without letting me know, and I'm left to dispose of their belongings."

"Could someone have stolen your key to the newspaper office?"

"Well . . . I suppose so." Mr. Spaulding opened a desk drawer, then shook his head. "Oh, Lord. Yes. It's gone." He pressed his fingers to his forehead. His skin had a pasty look. "This whole venture is turning into a disaster."

His air of defeat annoyed Emma. Thunderation, didn't she have enough to worry about? "Mr. Spaulding, is there a—a sheriff in town? Someone who can help us?"

He shook his head. "No. Closest one's in Denver City. A dying little place like this—we're on our own."

On our own. Emma didn't like the sound of that, and her voice came out sharper than she'd intended. "Well, we'll have to take care of things ourselves, then. Mother just hired a big Negro man named Mule Tom to help with the press and to guard the shop at night. But we'll still need a new padlock."

"Of course." Mr. Spaulding stared dully at his desk. "Stop at the store and tell Mr. Boggs to put it on my account."

Emma found Mr. Boggs unpacking a crate of skillets. "Every man heading to the goldfields needs a good fry pan," he said cheerfully. "What can I do for you, Emma?"

"We've had trouble at the print shop, and we need a new padlock." She told him what had happened.

"I'm sorry to hear that." He ran a hand over his bald head. "And I heard about the fire yesterday. You ladies have had a string of bad luck, that's for certain sure."

It's more than bad luck, Emma thought. She leaned on the counter as he fetched a new padlock. Two keys were tied to it with a twist of wire.

"Want me to wrap this up for you?" Mr. Boggs asked.

"No, I—" Emma caught her breath. "Why, that's it!"

"Begging your pardon?"

Emma pointed at the big roll of brown wrapping paper behind the counter. "Can we have some of your wrapping paper? To print the prospectus on? There's no other paper in town. I'm sure Mother or Mr. Spaulding will be able to replace whatever we use."

"But—it's brown. And heavier than newsprint. And in one big roll—"

"None of that matters!" Excitement bubbled inside Emma. "We can cut the paper down to size, and the black ink will still show up. Can we use it?"

Mr. Boggs folded his arms, looking baffled but pleased. "Well, sure! I'd be tickled to think I helped get *The Twin Pines Herald* off the ground."

Emma smacked the counter. One more problem solved.

❧

At the edge of town, Emma found the freight yard bustling. One of Mr. Torkelson's big blond sons was hitching a team of oxen to a massive wagon. A farmer pulled his own wagon into the yard. "I got thirty pounds of fleece I need carted to Golden," he shouted. "Where you want it unloaded?" Mr. Torkelson hurried from the office with a notebook in hand.

"May I bother you for a moment?" Emma asked, after the farmer had left. "I've got some good news. We're going to borrow some wrapping paper from the store. That will tide us over until the shipment of real newsprint arrives."

"Ya? That iss good news!" Mr. Torkelson grinned. "And your ink iss here."

"Wonderful!" Emma pulled her notebook and pencil from her pocket. "But I still have a couple more questions, for my article. Do you remember seeing anyone in the yard right before the fire?"

"Nobody in particular. I had joost gone inside. My boys did not see anything. My other hauler left for one of the ranches before the fire started."

"Can I talk to that man anyway?"

Mr. Torkelson shrugged. "When he gets back. He headed out on an overnight run this morning."

Crackers. No help there. "Nobody else was around?"

"Well . . . a few. People waiting for Lars to unload something of theirs, ya?"

"Was Dixie John one of them?" Emma dared, trying to sound casual.

"Nah. He hass never hired me. Got nothing to haul, I'd say."

Emma sighed. This was getting her nowhere. "Well, the fire might have been an accident. Or someone might have started it deliberately. Can you think of anyone who might want to cause trouble?"

Mr. Torkelson looked bewildered. "But who would want that?"

"I don't know, Mr. Torkelson." Emma put her note-book away and managed a smile. "I was just asking."

Mr. Torkelson chuckled. "Miss Emma, you are going to be one good reporter. But this time, I think there iss joost no story."

Disappointed, Emma nodded and waved good-bye. What else could she do to find the troublemaker? She chewed that over as she headed back to the print shop. The attacks against the newspaper still made no sense.

Someone hollered behind her, and she stepped out of the way of a man leading a pack-mule train out of town. In addition to kegs and crates and even a tin coffeepot, each mule was hauling two planks of sawn lumber, the ends dragging in the dirt. Emma wondered if some mining-camp shack would be built from the lumber. Until arriving in Twin Pines, she'd never thought about everything that people living far from cities had to give up. Things like sawmills. And sheriffs. Mr. Spaulding's words echoed in her memory: *We're on our own.*

Emma pulled her notebook from her pocket and looked at her list of suspects: Dixie John, Blackjack, and Miss Amaretta. Emma couldn't imagine Miss Amaretta whistling outside her window! But . . . how could any of them be The Whistler? The Whistler had first appeared in Chicago. Emma didn't think any of her suspects had left Twin Pines long enough to make that trip. Besides, according to their stagecoach driver, the strange man

asking about Emma and Mother along the trail had a
limp. Neither Dixie John nor Blackjack limped. Had The
Whistler been *sent* by one of them? The whistling had
begun the day Mother received Mr. Spaulding's job offer.

Below her list of suspects, Emma wrote, *Who is
The Whistler?*

Emma swallowed hard, tapping the page with her
pencil, as a cold breath slid down her collar. She knew
what she needed to do. Tonight, if The Whistler made
another appearance, she would be waiting.

CHAPTER 7

NEW RESOLVE

I think I'll keep both of these," Mother said, pocketing the two keys to their new padlock. "Mr. Spaulding means well, but I honestly don't know how that man thought he could ever build a town. He doesn't have the sense of a goose."

Remembering how dejected Mr. Spaulding had looked, Emma changed the subject. "Mother, I have good news. I found some paper! Mr. Boggs said we could use his big roll of wrapping paper!"

Mother paused, a finger on her chin. "Wrapping paper. Yes, that could work. Our prospectus will look odd, but that's no matter. Yes." She nodded with more enthusiasm. "Yes, indeed! Emma, you're brilliant!"

A glow spread like warm honey through Emma. But she didn't have much time to enjoy it, for Mother went to work like a whirlwind. She and Mule Tom had carefully retrieved all of the jumbled type from the sawdust, and

Emma went back to work—*again*—sorting it by letters and sizes. Mother sent Mule Tom to retrieve the heavy roll of paper, and then to the freight office for the waiting keg of ink. When Jeremy arrived, Mother set him to work measuring and cutting the wrapping paper into press-sized pieces.

Once the typecases were finally organized, Mother set the type herself, snatching each needed letter from the typecase and shaping the pieces into words and sentences. Her speed was astonishing, especially since the type had to be inserted into the tray backward so that it would print correctly when applied to the paper! She used a type stick to make straight lines and kept her articles handy for reference. "You'll catch on," Mother said when she noticed Emma staring. "It just takes practice."

By late afternoon they were ready to begin printing. Mother showed Jeremy how to moisten each piece of paper with a sponge and how to ink the waiting type. Mule Tom claimed the exhausting job of tugging the lever Mr. Abbott had carved, which brought the paper and inked type together. Emma strung thin cord back and forth above their heads and draped each printed piece of paper over it to dry. They repeated the entire process for the reverse side of the paper.

"I never knew printing a newspaper was such hard work," Jeremy sighed as the sun began to slip behind the mountains.

"Be glad this is just a single sheet," Emma muttered. "When we print the full newspapers, each sheet has to be hand-folded and the crease pressed in with a whalebone."

He shrugged. "Well, it's better than digging fence-post holes for my father. Mrs. Henderson, sorry, but I gotta go. I've got evening chores waiting."

Mother looked startled. "My goodness, is it suppertime already? Emma, would you run and ask Mrs. Sloane if she'd be so kind as to let you bring supper over in a pail?"

Jeremy and Emma walked together as far as the boardinghouse. "I never met anyone like your mother before," Jeremy said.

"She loved helping at my father's newspaper office. And during the war, she worked for the Sanitary Commission. She likes having a job to do." Emma tried to keep any hint of resentment from her voice.

"She sure works hard." Jeremy's tone was admiring.

"Well, she wanted to print three hundred copies of the prospectus. She won't stop until she gets it done."

Emma's prediction came true. After she, Mother, and Mule Tom split a dubious dinner of fried doughnuts and cold beef stew, Mother hung two lanterns from the rafters and they went back to work. Emma helped until her eyes felt sandy and the muscles between her shoulder blades ached. "Mother," she said finally, "I need to go to bed."

"Oh, Emma!" Mother darted from the press and gave her a quick hug. "Of course, dear. You've been simply wonderful today." Then she hesitated. "I *would* like to finish up here, though. Would you mind horribly going back by yourself?"

Emma sighed. She'd spent the day watching Mother stride back and forth in her ridiculous trousers, overseeing her inexperienced workers, greeting the occasional patron who stopped by to ask questions or pay for a subscription. Mother's hair had straggled down from its bun, and her left cheek was streaked with ink. And she was happy.

"No, Mother," Emma said. "I don't mind going on alone."

She walked back to the boardinghouse as the last blues of twilight shadowed the garbage in the streets. Emma was fiercely proud that they'd managed to print the prospectus. Still, loneliness nibbled. Emma couldn't help remembering all the times when Mother's war work had consumed all else: "Emma dear, we want to get the hall decorated for the donation party tonight. Would you mind horribly having dinner with the Littletons again?" Or, "I'd love to look at your sketchbook, darling, but can it wait? I'm scheduled to meet with the contractor about the floral pavilion for the Sanitary Fair."

A man coughed somewhere behind Emma, and she cast a nervous glance over her shoulder into the deepening shadows. Was The Whistler watching her? Maybe even *following* her? Didn't Mother worry about Emma walking back alone? Emma had to remind herself, in fairness, that Mother didn't know The Whistler had appeared in Twin Pines. Still, Emma walked back to the boarding-house as fast as she could.

In their bedroom, Emma lit a lamp and sat staring at the photograph of her father. If only he hadn't died, if only the dreadful Civil War had never started . . .

Emma gave herself a mental shake. She wasn't sure Father would approve of this Colorado venture, but he would want Emma to help Mother in any way she could. And, after all, Mother's absence tonight made Emma's plan to catch The Whistler much easier.

Emma washed her face and tidied the room. Then she dimmed the lamp, tiptoed downstairs, and eased into a chair by the front parlor window. If The Whistler followed the pattern of the last two evenings, he would soon appear, whistling *Maggie by My Side*.

Who would she see? Emma rubbed her arms. If she could catch sight of him right here in the middle of town, with Mrs. Sloane and The Raven's patrons within holler-ing distance, maybe she'd have the courage to confront him. If she didn't recognize him, she'd demand to know who he was and why he was trying so hard to scare the Hendersons out of Twin Pines.

Laughter and shouting drifted across the street from the saloon. Emma heard several horses trotting by, and the rattle of a wagon. A man leaving the saloon cursed roundly when he stumbled down the steps. But as the minutes stretched into an hour, Emma did *not* hear a man whistling.

Frustration and disappointment welled in her throat. Finally, when she couldn't stay awake any longer, Emma gave up and went to bed.

⌒ᗒ

"Look at this," Mother said triumphantly. Early-morning sun slanted across piles of the brown prospectus, stacked on one of the print shop's worktables. "Three hundred of them."

"Great guns!" Jeremy exclaimed. "That's wonderful!"

"Yes, ma'am," Mule Tom echoed more quietly.

Emma picked up one of the papers. "The Twin Pines Herald" marched across the top in big print. The front page contained subscription and advertising information, as well as Mother's article about the stolen press handle and the burned paper shipment. The right-hand column, labeled "Local Items," featured tidbits Emma had gathered while soliciting subscriptions: *Mrs. Handshew recently became a grandmother. Mr. Taylor is recovering from a bad cough. Jim Moody had Dixie John dig a new well on his ranch.*

"I predict that every one of those people will subscribe to the paper, if they haven't already." Mother grinned. "People love seeing their names in print. Your father taught me that, Emma."

As Emma and Jeremy headed out for a morning of

distributing the prospectus and soliciting subscriptions, Jeremy scrunched one hand down into a pocket. "I got something for you," he said.

He laughed at her expression when he plopped a rock into her palm—a rough, egg-shaped, mud-colored rock. "Take it home and hit it with a mallet."

"Um . . . all right. Thank you." Emma slipped the rock into her own pocket, suddenly missing Judith terribly. This was no doubt some mineralogical treasure that Jeremy had found. But minerals didn't interest Emma, and this particular rock was as ugly as the rest of Twin Pines.

Jeremy had driven a light wagon to town that morning. "I told Pa that you and I need to travel out to some of the farms today," he said as he helped her clamber up to the seat. "We'll cover more ground this way." He picked up the lines and clucked to the mare.

They dropped off stacks of the prospectus at the boardinghouse, Mr. Boggs's store, and the land office. Jeremy even left some at The Raven before they headed north into the long valley that cradled Twin Pines.

"Twin Pines is at the southern end of the valley," he told Emma. "Mr. Spaulding bought land up to the northern end, about four miles from here. There are three farms up there, ours and two others, all strung along the creek. It's good land. We do better than the farmers down on the plains. We get more rain from those showers that come over the mountains."

Rocky foothills bounded the valley on both sides. The pretty, rolling meadow Jeremy drove through bore no resemblance to the desert Emma had seen in eastern Colorado—or to the scarred slopes around Twin Pines, which were studded with tree stumps left by men hastily building cabins and chopping firewood and which were grazed to stubble by the pack mules and freight oxen.

"It's so green here!" Emma sighed.

Jeremy smiled. "My ma called this Peaceful Valley—Oh, say! Did you see that wild canary? They're a sight. And see that swale? My pa shot an elk there last winter. The snows force 'em down from the high mountains."

It grew hot, riding in the open wagon without shade. But Jeremy was a lively guide, and so much green eased something tight inside Emma. Jeremy showed her how the cottonwood trees marked the creek—"footprints of the river," he called them—and carpets of blanketflowers and larkspur took her breath away. "Perhaps I can pick some later to arrange for a still-life painting," she said. "I haven't touched my paints since we arrived."

When they reached a pass that angled away from the main valley, Jeremy turned off. "There are a few ranches tucked up in some of the higher draws—"

"Draws?" Emma wrinkled her forehead.

"Small canyons. They weren't part of Mr. Spaulding's land, but we'll still want to visit the folks who live there."

That morning they visited five bachelor brothers, a

family with three little girls wearing identical dresses, and a man with a scraggly black beard who talked enthusiastically about running cattle. By the time Jeremy and Emma circled back to Peaceful Valley, the sun was high overhead.

"Now we're back on Mr. Spaulding's land," Jeremy told her. "We'll head south again past the three farms. My pa bought the one closest to Twin Pines. A family from Ohio bought this far one." He pointed to a log home squatting near a field already reclaimed by weeds. "They gave up and sold the land back to Mr. Spaulding again, so it's empty." Jeremy stared grimly at the forlorn farmyard for a moment, then slapped the reins against the horse's back. "Pa said somebody new just settled on the middle place, though," he told Emma. "We should visit there. We can stop at my place after that if you're getting hungry."

"I'm just thirsty." Emma tilted her straw hat against the sun's glare. Sweat trickled down her neck.

A few minutes later, they approached a tiny cabin made of black logs, roofed with a haphazard pile of pine boughs heaped on a framework of poles. A blanket served as a door, weighted at the bottom with rocks to keep it from flapping. A young woman in a faded dress and limp sunbonnet was scratching in a big garden beside the cabin.

This stop is surely a waste of time, Emma thought. Since coming to Colorado, she'd met many people who barely had a pot to stew chicken in. But this place smelled of pure and absolute desperation.

As Emma and Jeremy climbed from the wagon, the woman dropped the hoe and bounded to greet them. She didn't look more than a few years older than Emma. Her face was hatchet-thin and dotted with freckles in spite of the tunnel-like sunbonnet. "Hello! I'm Tildy Pearce." Tildy surprised Emma by pumping her hand.

Emma introduced herself and Jeremy with a tongue dry enough to rattle in her mouth. "Do you mind if we get a drink from your well?" she asked.

"I wouldn't mind—if I *had* a well. Found one half-dug when we got here, and never got around to finishing the job. But I've got a bucket of water hauled up fresh from the creek."

Emma gulped the contents of the tin cup thrust into her hand. Then she explained about the newspaper and brought out a copy of the prospectus. "You're welcome to look at it." Her cheeks grew hot—did Tildy even know how to read?

But Tildy snatched it from her hand. "A *newspaper!*" she breathed, as if Emma had offered something holy. "I've been so yearning for something to read!" She scanned the page, then looked at Emma and Jeremy with delight. "Can you come inside? I'll show you something."

The only light in the cabin trickled through the stove-pipe hole, which was too large for the stovepipe itself.

The room smelled of rancid pork. As Emma's eyes adjusted, she made out a reddish-colored, rickety bed banged together from skinny logs and pieces of a packing box. A rocking chair had been fashioned from a barrel. An oiled wagon cover served as carpet, and wide strips of muslin were tacked along the pole ceiling—obviously to keep dirt from sifting down.

Tildy noted Emma's stare. "I hope to do better by fall," she said apologetically, gesturing toward the filthy muslin. "Critters get in there and nest. I'm trying to save enough money to order me some good boards. But look here." She pointed at the bed. "I fixed that up myself. Looks like cherry, don't it? I had a bit of brick dust left—I brought it for scouring—and mixed it with linseed oil to make the stain. I think it looks pretty."

"Yes." Emma swallowed. "It does. Tildy, are you here all by yourself?" She didn't see evidence of anyone else.

"Well, just after me and my husband settled here, he got gold fever and headed up into the hills. Said he'd be gone a day or two, just scouting things out. But he hasn't been back."

"I'm so sorry." Emma didn't know what else to say.

"I'm making on all right. He weren't the best husband anyway. I guess I'd be handling most of the work one way or the other." Tildy reached to a high shelf behind the stove. "Here's what I wanted to show you. I've been reading this book every evening I can, after chores are done. It's a blessing to have it, but I surely would covet getting an honest newspaper every now and again." Glowing with pride, she handed Emma the book.

Webster's *Elementary Speller.* Emma stared at the worn book, imagining Tildy Pearce huddled by her stove in the evening, straining to read the only thing she had for company—a spelling book. Emma tried to smile as she handed it back. Tildy put her treasured book on its shelf and led the way back into the sunshine.

Emma chewed her lip. "Tildy—I'll make sure you get a subscription to the newspaper." Would a free subscription offend Tildy? But surely Tildy couldn't afford it herself! Emma thought Mother would understand.

But Tildy already had things figured out. "You get my name on the list, or whatever. I can get the money. I walk into town some evenings, if I'm not too worn out. At The Raven, there's always men who'll pay for a dance. Oh, wait!"

Tildy darted inside and came out again with a piece of paper in her hand. "I've been puzzling over something. Maybe you or your mother could help me out." She pushed the paper into Emma's hand. "My husband bought this land proper from Mr. Spaulding. I saw the money pass hands. And Mr. Spaulding gave us this."

Emma skimmed the writing. "It's your receipt for the land payment. It proves that you paid Mr. Spaulding."

Tildy nodded. "Yes. But shouldn't we also have gotten another piece of paper—the deed to the land?"

"Um . . . I don't know exactly how that works." Emma glanced at Jeremy, who didn't seem to know either. "But I can ask my mother. She knows a lot about business." She handed the receipt back to Tildy.

"I'd surely appreciate that." Tildy stepped back from the wagon. "And tell her I'll be waiting to get the first full issue of her newspaper! I can see myself getting through the winter, even, with a fresh newspaper to read every week or so."

As she and Jeremy headed back to town, Emma tried to imagine how tired she would feel if she spent the day doing farm labor, then walked several miles to town and danced with a bunch of boisterous miners, then walked home again.

The newspaper was more than a way to share information. Even more than a way to "boom the town," as the men called it, and attract new settlers. For the first time, Emma realized what the newspaper would mean to people like Tildy, or to lonely miners trying to earn enough money to fetch their families from the East, cut off from companionship and books.

And she thought again of The Whistler—or whoever was trying so hard to frighten her and Mother into quitting.

"I'll tell you one thing, Jeremy," she said, as they rounded a hill and the forlorn roofline of Twin Pines came into sight. "*The Twin Pines Herald* is *not* going to fail."

CHAPTER 8
THE RAVEN

Little Josephine Ellis narrowly avoided heartbreak when she dropped a penny on the boardwalk on Thursday in front of Mr. Boggs's store and it fell through a crack. Mr. Boggs pulled up a board and fetched it for her.

"That's a good start," Mother said, leaning over Emma's shoulder late that afternoon. "But see if you can write the same story using fewer words— Oh! Mule Tom, let me see how that looks." Mother hurried to the print shop's worktable to check Mr. Boggs's advertising broadsides.

Emma scowled at her notebook. Her children's news column was boring. Besides, she couldn't concentrate. Suppose The Whistler was planning his next attack on the newspaper—right this moment? Would he set the office on fire? Shoot through a window? Emma fought off a wave of panic. Mule Tom's low murmur was reassuring. Thank heavens for Mule Tom!

Emma turned to her notes about possible trouble-makers. Waiting for The Whistler to appear last night hadn't gotten her anywhere. It was time to take the next step, a good reporter step: ask questions.

But nerves curled in the pit of her belly. She couldn't very well sit at the breakfast table and interview Blackjack and Dixie John, could she? She needed to talk to each man separately. And that meant going into The Raven, where each man seemed to spend most of his waking hours.

Emma sighed. She wished Jeremy hadn't headed home for chores. Maybe—

"Mrs. Henderson!" Miss Amaretta Holly stood in the doorway, clutching a copy of the prospectus. Two bright spots of red burned in her cheeks.

"Miss Holly?" Mother edged around the bulky press. "What can I do—"

"You can explain this!" Miss Amaretta advanced and slapped the brown paper on the table. One slender finger jabbed a column on the back page. "As editor, you're expected to—to share *news*! Not persuade others to adopt your own peculiar habits!"

Emma knew what Miss Amaretta was unhappy about. Mother had included a short notice:

> *Ladies: Womanly manners do not demand a skirt trailing in the filth. Skirts hemmed to a reasonable length are no more than a sensible health precaution.*

And for women working on farms or ranches or
in the goldfields, a Reform Dress is beyond value
in comfort and convenience. For particulars, visit
the editor.

"I think I'll check on that paper shipment now,"
Mule Tom muttered. He touched his hat politely to
each of the women, then escaped the shack.

"Why don't we sit down," Mother said calmly, indicating two chairs by the worktable. "And Emma, would
you please make some tea?"

Emma crouched by the tiny cast-iron stove. After
lighting a new blaze, she fiddled with the stove dampers,
filled the tin coffeepot with water, and set it over the
firebox. All the while, she listened to Mother and
Miss Amaretta.

"... and I am making progress!" Miss Amaretta
was saying. "When I arrived, Mr. Spaulding—our town
father—spent his evenings at The Raven, gambling and
drinking. He hasn't set foot in the saloon in weeks. I've
helped him see the value of setting a decent example
for the rest of our citizens."

"But what has that to do with me?" Mother asked.

"It's bad enough that you choose to dress in an—an
unconventional manner. But I never dreamed that you
would use your newspaper to encourage other women
to do the same!" Miss Amaretta pressed her fingertips

to her temples. "You are urging women to abandon their womanly callings—"

"I'm doing no such thing," Mother interrupted, kindly but firmly. "I also printed a recipe for mutton stew and advice for cleaning grease from linen. And my editorial called for a proper town dump, so that we won't have to wade through filth and rubbish in the streets. Surely you don't find fault with those things." Mother's eyes flashed as she made her points, but she punctuated her sentences with smiles. *She's enjoying this,* Emma realized with a start. Mother wasn't nervous anymore.

"Let me tell you about something that happened to me," Mother said. Her gaze darted to her copy of Father's daguerreotype, which watched over the print shop from a high shelf. "About a month after Emma and I learned that my husband had been killed, I received a letter from a soldier who had served with him. Miss Holly, the letter contained a proposal of marriage. I'd never even met this man!"

What? Emma had never heard that before!

"It was a very respectful letter," Mother continued. "He was most sincere. Fortunately, my husband left us a little money, and I knew that I could provide for Emma and myself with my ability as a newspaperwoman, so I wrote the man back and very gently declined his most kind offer. But don't you see, many women wouldn't have had that option! It made me terribly sad to think that such a letter would have been the answer to many a desperate widow's prayers. Our society forces women to depend on men for almost everything. All I'm trying to do is help women understand that they do indeed have choices in life."

"But I support myself as well," Miss Amaretta objected. "And I haven't set aside my womanliness to do so."

Mother's eyes sparked. "With all due respect, most women haven't the luxury of your occupation! How many dressmakers does Twin Pines need? Most of the women hereabouts are doing hard work on ranches or working themselves to nubs over laundry kettles. Why should they be hampered by tight corsets and hems they trip over?"

Emma stared at her fingers, thinking about Tildy Pearce. Maybe if Tildy had a Reform Dress, just to wear when she was doing carpentry work or plowing a field . . . well, maybe that wouldn't be such a horrible thing.

Miss Amaretta had leaned closer to Mother, as if about to share a secret. "Mrs. Henderson, you and Emma haven't been here very long. Let me give you some advice. I've found that holding myself as a lady offers me protection from the roughest men. I'm afraid that the women most likely to receive insults are those who somehow invite them. I know that you've had some troubles with the newspaper. Perhaps—"

"Are you suggesting that I've brought those troubles upon myself?" Mother demanded. "Why—"

"Water's hot!" Emma announced. She used a thick square of wool to pull the pot from the stove and set it on the table. She snatched mugs and tea from the little shelf where Mother had secured the fixings for snacks, and plunked them by the pot. Then she smiled with forced cheer at both women. "Mother, I'm going to ... to ... talk to some more people about subscriptions." She grabbed her notebook and fled.

Outside, she paused to draw a deep breath. Crackers! She hated these arguments. She felt slammed in the middle.

Well. She set her shoulders, considering. Clouds cloaked the sun, and a late-afternoon shower was threatening. Not a good time to range too far afield. With a sigh, she turned toward the saloon. Time to get on with business.

⚓

Emma paused in front of The Raven, trying to scrape up the nerve to enter the saloon. She stood beneath the overhanging roof, watching raindrops splatter the street. The grating scratch of an ill-played fiddle drifted through the opening above the swinging doors, punctuated by bursts of laughter. She glanced down the street toward the news-paper office. No sign of Miss Amaretta yet. Emma surely didn't want Miss Amaretta to see her enter the saloon. Taking a deep breath, she plunged inside.

Emma half expected to be shouted back outside where

she belonged, but no one seemed to notice her. As her eyes adjusted to the dimness, she looked around the big room and saw perhaps a dozen men sitting at round wooden tables with cards in their hands and piles of little porcelain disks in front of them. They're *gambling,* Emma realized with horrified fascination. She'd once heard her minister in Chicago call gambling the devil's business. It didn't look like much, actually, and she felt a little let down.

A bar stretched along the right wall, holding plates of roast beef and crackers and hard-boiled eggs. A shelf of tin cups and glasses and bottles ran behind the bar. Signs tacked to the wall said *PAY AS YOU GO* and *NO TRUST* and *25 CENTS A DRINK*. Half a dozen men lounged along the bar, and a man behind it was pouring someone a drink.

Emma jumped when someone tugged her sleeve. "Beg pardon, miss," a young man asked eagerly. He held his felt hat politely in his hands. "Are you here to dance?" He nodded toward the fiddle player mangling another tune. "Fifty cents?"

"No! I—that is, no thank you," Emma stammered. "I was looking for Mr. Blackjack." Dixie John would do, too, but she wanted to start with the more civil of the two men.

"Oh." The man's face fell, but he pointed. "There he is."

Emma turned and saw Blackjack emerging from a door she hadn't noticed before, near the back of the saloon. He surveyed the room and, for the briefest moment, looked startled to see Emma. His habitual small smile slid back into place as he approached. "Why, Miss Henderson! What brings you here? Come to solicit a subscription, perhaps?"

Emma wished she could guess what he was thinking. "Do you want to subscribe to *The Herald*?" she asked, slipping her notebook and pencil from her pocket.

"Why, of course! Please put me down for an annual subscription. Have your mother send me a bill."

"I will." She made the note. Mother preferred payment in advance, but Emma didn't want to argue with Blackjack—not when her stomach was already fluttering. "I'm glad to hear that you want to subscribe. I had thought—that is, I wondered . . ." He raised one eyebrow. *Stop yammering!* Emma ordered herself. She forced the words out. "Mr. Blackjack, is there a quiet place where I could ask you a couple of questions?"

"Why, certainly. My back room is free." If he was surprised by her request, he made no sign. Instead he led her through the door she'd noticed earlier, into a small room. A round gaming table stood in the center, but unlike those in the main saloon, this one was covered by an elegant paisley cloth edged with fringe. Curtains of the same fabric adorned the single, rain-streaked window. Next to the window, a door in the back wall led outside. Several tidy decks of cards and stacks of the round porcelain gambling disks waited on a sideboard beside two glass decanters and crystal glasses.

Emma sat in the chair Blackjack offered and poised her pencil, trying to sound businesslike. "Sir, we like to collect news from all the businesses in town. Is there anything you'd like to share?"

Blackjack spread his hands. "Can't say I have a story for you. Business is good."

Emma took a deep breath and screwed up her courage. "Mr. Blackjack, on our first morning here, Dixie John accused you of cheating. Do you . . . that is . . ."

"Why, Miss Henderson, are you asking me if I run an honest business?" He threw his head back and laughed. "Just put it this way. My enterprise would collapse if my customers didn't want to return."

"That's not really an answer," Emma muttered, scribbling furiously.

Blackjack leaned on his elbows. "My dear Emma. May I call you Emma? I'm starting to understand what you're getting at. I have, of course, heard about the . . . *difficulties* you and your mother have encountered. And you are no doubt wondering if whoever is behind the attacks on your newspaper is someone with something to hide."

His smile made Emma's skin crawl. Coming into this private room with him hadn't been wise. Her gaze darted to the open door. The sound of laughter was welcome.

"Let me put your mind at ease, Emma. I have no reason to fear your little newspaper."

That *little* grated Emma's nerves. "This may be a joke to

you," Emma said. "But a lot of people believe the whole town will fail without a newspaper to attract new settlers."

Blackjack shook his head. "The truth is, it doesn't matter to me. Don't you see? This saloon—it's just a building. I'd lose money if I had to abandon it, but not enough to cause me serious harm. My business skills can go anywhere—if not Twin Pines, then the next town. So, my dear, I'm afraid you're looking in the wrong place. I have nothing to hide from a journalist, and no reason to care if your newspaper lives or dies."

Well! What a nasty man!

Blackjack leaned forward. "Emma, let me give you some advice. This is a rough town. Many men would not look . . . kindly on a young woman poking her nose into their business. I suggest you stop now, before you find yourself in real trouble."

Was that truly advice? Or a threat? The air felt suddenly cold. "Thank you for your time," Emma said stiffly, jumping to her feet. Blackjack made a formal bow.

As Emma emerged into the main saloon, someone called her name. At least, she thought it was her name. "Miz—Hendershun. Hender—Hendershun." Dixie John was slumped at a table near the door to the back room, his hat pulled low on his forehead. Emma had been so eager to escape from Blackjack's smug smile and veiled threats that she'd forgotten she'd meant to interview Dixie John, too! She hesitated.

"Come 'ere." He beckoned.

Emma stepped closer. Whatever was in the big tin cup on the table in front of him smelled bad. *He* smelled bad.

"I heard what you shed. What you *said*."

He's drunk! Emma realized with disgust. She took a step back.

"No, wait." Dixie John held up one trembling hand. "I know."

"You know what?" Emma asked impatiently.

"What—cher—*lookin'* for," he got out, as if she was an incredibly stupid girl who required great patience. "I dug too good, you shee." He took another swallow from his cup and wiped his mouth with the back of his hand.

"Excuse me," Emma muttered, but Dixie John managed to grab her wrist. "Itsh the gold!" he muttered. "You won't believe me. But id—itsh all there. You can find it. You have to look ish . . . *ish* . . . th' bird's eye—"

Blackjack's hand dropped onto Dixie John's shoulder. "I suspect Miss Emma has business elsewhere, my friend," he said pleasantly. "And you are in no condition to talk with young ladies." He nodded toward the door. "Go on," he told Emma. "He won't bother you. He always rambles when he's drunk."

Emma wrenched her hand free and fled.

CHAPTER 9
THE WHISTLER

 s she bolted from the saloon, Emma almost plowed into Tildy Pearce. "Oh!" Emma exclaimed. "I beg your pardon!"

Tildy's tired eyes squinted into a smile. "I was so excited about meetin' you this morning, I decided to head in early to make me some money." She cocked her head toward the sound of the fiddle.

"Tildy . . ." Emma hesitated. The skin on her wrist felt itchy where Dixie John had held it. "Is it safe for you to be in the saloon? I mean—some of the men get drunk."

"Most of the men are just lonely," Tildy said with a shrug. "I keep away from the heavy gamblers. They're the only ones to cause trouble. A man in debt is a desperate man."

"Well, good luck," Emma said, not sure what else to say. "And oh—I haven't forgotten about your land deed. I'll ask my mother tonight." She watched as Tildy disappeared into The Raven, ready to dance the evening away.

The rain had stopped, and Emma held her skirt out
of the mud as she hurried back to the newspaper office.
Blackjack's threat and Dixie John's ramblings made her
uneasy. The haunting whistled strains of *Maggie by My Side*
echoed through her mind. When a passing man nodded
politely in greeting, she jerked away, then forced herself to
take a deep breath. It was suddenly hard to tell what was
real and whom to trust.

She found her mother and Mule Tom bent over the
printing press. "Oh, Emma, there you are," Mother said.
"I was hoping you'd get back before I had to leave. Jeremy's
father and Mr. Boggs and some of the other men are
forming a Safety Committee, since we don't have a sheriff
yet. They're meeting tonight in the room above Mr. Boggs's
store. I've been invited to attend and write a story about
it. Do you want to come?"

Emma considered. This would be the first formal
gathering Mother attended in her Reform Dress. Heaven
only knew what reaction that would provoke! "I don't
think so. When are you going?"

"In just a few minutes."

"Mother! It's almost suppertime!"

"You don't mind going back by yourself, do you?"
Mother asked.

Yes! Emma wanted to say. *Yes, I do mind. I always mind
when your work is more important than me! Especially when
scary things are happening!* But the words wouldn't come out.

Mother bit her lip. "Emma, I won't always work so hard," she said after a moment. "I promise! But I want this story in the first edition of the paper, so we can send it off with Mr. Abbott's brother when he heads back east. This first edition is so important, Emma! Once it's done . . ."

Emma nodded. She *knew* how important the first edition was. But she also knew that after that, other things would become just as urgent for Mother. There was no point making that observation, so she changed the subject. "Mother, I need to ask you something. I met a young woman today—Tildy Pearce. She wants to subscribe to the paper so badly that she's selling dances at The Raven to earn the money."

"Gracious!" Mother's eyebrows raised.

"She and her husband bought some farmland from Mr. Spaulding. She has a receipt proving that they paid him for the land, but nothing else. She thinks she should have a deed to the land."

"Yes, that's right." Mother nodded. "Mr. Spaulding forgot to give it to her, no doubt. That man has the business sense of a caterpillar. She needs to press him on it, as I've had to do on the things he promised me."

"I'll tell her." Thinking of Tildy Pearce, gamely bobbing up and down in some lonely miner's arms on the dance floor, made Emma want to do whatever she could to help.

Mother pulled her cape from the peg by the door. "Thank you for your help today, Mule Tom," she called,

and to Emma she said, "Come along, dear. I'll walk as
far as the boardinghouse with you."

After Mother headed off to her meeting, Emma
sat down to a miserable supper of beans and bacon in
Mrs. Sloane's dining room. Resentment simmered inside
as Emma picked at her food. Living in a boardinghouse
meant Mother never had to fix meals, and she'd hired a
laundress to wash their clothes once a week. *Living here
makes it too easy for Mother!* Emma thought. What if Mother
decided she and Emma didn't need a house after all?

At least Dixie John didn't show up for supper.
Blackjack nodded pleasantly at Emma, then spent much
of the meal sparring with Miss Amaretta. A man called
Spuddy, who peddled supplies to distant mining camps,
was also spending the night, and he talked nonstop about
the need for decent roads into the mountains. Emma was
glad to escape to her bedroom.

Once there, she sat down at the desk with her notebook. She hadn't learned anything useful that afternoon.
Blackjack talked in circles. As for Dixie John . . . Emma
shuddered as she remembered the smell of strong drink
on his breath. What a horrible man! Surely she couldn't
put any stock in his drunken ramblings.

Could she?

Emma forced herself to recall their conversation. Most
of what he said hadn't made any sense. Still, he had tried
to tell her *something.* Could she afford to overlook that?

Closing her eyes, she listened again to his words exactly as she remembered them, then struggled to write them down. A bunch of nonsense! *Itsh the gold! You won't believe me. But id—itsh all there. You can find it. You have to look ish . . . ish . . . th' bird's eye—*

"'You can find it,'" she muttered, staring at the page. "'Look *ish*' . . . look *with* the bird's eye? Look *in* the bird's eye?" She snorted. What in thunderation did he mean?

She chewed on the end of the pencil, then wrote *Bird's-eye map?* Was Dixie John referring to the beautiful map hanging in Mr. Spaulding's office? What else could he have meant? She stared out the window, puzzling over the questions as she absently watched a cluster of men hurry up the steps of The Raven—

"Oh!" On the next line Emma wrote, *The Raven?* Could Dixie John have been referring to the saloon itself?

Something else nagged at the back of her mind. Emma curled up in the chair, hugging her knees, as she tried to remember. Suddenly it came to her: Jeremy telling her about climbing the twin pines. "Climbs easy as a ladder," he'd said, "and you get an eagle's view once you're up a ways."

Was that what Dixie John had meant? That if she climbed the tree and looked down on the whole town, she'd see something important?

Emma stared at her notebook, trying to make sense of her ideas. Finally she shoved it away. "This is all nonsense!" she muttered, feeling foolish for even trying to make sense of a drunken man's ramblings. In the morning, if Dixie John showed up for breakfast and seemed sober, she'd just ask him.

After washing her face and visiting the outhouse, Emma was reaching for her nightgown when her hand stilled. Should she try to wait for The Whistler again? She eyed her bed wistfully. It had been a long day, and she was tired.

She decided to curl up in the chair by her own window instead of waiting downstairs. She was turning over the exchange with Dixie John in her mind when she dozed off.

Whistled notes slid through the night like a ghost, jolting her awake. *Maggie by My Side.*

Avoiding the window, Emma shot to her feet, raced through the hall, and skittered down the stairs. The last notes of the chorus reached her ears as she fumbled with the front door. She didn't want to scare The Whistler away! Then she slipped into the damp night air, heart pounding.

The whistling had stopped. Emma darted onto the boardwalk just in time to see a shadowy figure disappearing down the street, away from the more permanent buildings. Laughter spilled from The Raven, and a horse tied to the hitching rail out front snorted impatiently. No one else was in sight. Emma turned to follow the man.

The saloon glowed with lamplight, as did the meeting room above Mr. Boggs's store, and some of the miners camped near the creek had lit a small bonfire. Most of the town, however, was dark. Following the man away from the lively oasis of The Raven, Emma felt another flicker of unease. *I shouldn't be doing this,* she thought—but she couldn't bear to give up now, not when she was so close.

The man had a good head start, but her prickling nerves warned her to move stealthily, keeping to the shadows. As she closed the gap, she noted that he was short and slightly built—and that he walked with a limp. Emma felt a sudden sheen of sweat on her skin. Surely this was the man who'd asked about the Hendersons during their journey west!

The Whistler led her toward the outskirts of Twin Pines, where the scattered cabins and tents were shadowed and silent. Emma's footsteps slowed. The half-moon slid behind a cloak of clouds, and the saloon noise had faded behind her. A sudden snarl split the night. Emma almost jumped from her skin. *It's just a couple of dogs fighting over an antelope bone,* she told herself, but when one of the creatures slunk away from the shadow of a tiny cabin, she saw that it was a coyote instead. She stifled a cry and scurried backward.

The Whistler had melted into the shadows, but Emma couldn't will her feet to follow. An icy finger of fear traced down her spine. For a moment Emma stood rooted in the road, heart hammering. Then she snatched up her skirts and fled back to the boardinghouse.

Chapter 10

A Likely Suspect

Emma woke the next morning very annoyed with herself. *I was so close!* she fumed. *Twice* yesterday she'd gotten spooked—once in the saloon when Dixie John was holding her wrist, and later following The Whistler. Her father had faced battle without running away! Surely she could have done better.

Mother, who had slipped into bed long after Emma had curled lonely and cold under the covers, didn't notice Emma's mood. "The meeting was interesting," she chattered as she pulled on her chemise. "I need to determine how much space we have left in the newspaper for the story. You can help me. Now—what do you think? Are you willing to wear your Reform Dress today?"

"*No!*"

Mother frowned. "Please change your tone, Emma. What has you in such a nettle this morning?"

Emma twisted her mouth. Part of her longed to tell

Mother that The Whistler was in Twin Pines. But Mother
would surely scold Emma for not telling her sooner—and
especially for trying to follow him alone. Emma was in no
mood for a scolding. "Nothing," she said finally. Mother
cocked one eyebrow but let her be.

Breakfast consisted of sourdough pancakes, stewed
dried apples, and viciously strong coffee. Spuddy, the
traveling peddler, started an argument by demanding that
Mother write an editorial against the proposed treaty
between the government and the Cheyenne and Arapaho
Indians. "We need to run them from the territory!" he
exclaimed. His poorly-dried deerskin suit rattled like old
peapods with every indignant jab of his finger. "And the
Utes, too!"

"As I understand it, our army committed a massacre
at Sand Creek in 1864," Mother shot back. "I will not use
my newspaper to promote such outrages . . ."

Emma watched Spuddy's face turn brick red. *Lovely,* she
thought. Someone else who wasn't happy with *The Herald*'s
editor. The list seemed ever-growing.

On Emma's other side, Miss Amaretta launched a
genteel assault on Blackjack's line of business. "I suggest,"
she concluded, "that you spend some time reading the
Good Book instead of indulging in card games—"

"My dear Miss Holly." Blackjack smiled calmly.
"Wasn't it Paul the Apostle who said, 'Let the women
learn in silence. I suffer not a woman to teach, nor to

usurp authority over the man, but to be in silence—'"

"*Oh!*" Miss Amaretta's eyes glittered. "*Sir.* May I remind you . . ."

Emma was startled by a sudden revelation. In the heat of a good discussion, Miss Amaretta looked just like Mother. Some people might think arguing was unwomanly, but neither Mother nor Miss Amaretta backed off from a debate. Ha! Who'd have thought Miss Amaretta and Mother had anything in common?

The only person not engaged in discussion that morning was Dixie John. Emma eyed him over the rim of her coffee cup. His eyes looked bloodshot, and he winced whenever one of the arguments got too loud. Served him right for getting drunk yesterday! Still, Emma was glad when, amid the scrape of chairs and the din of closing conversations marking the end of the meal, she had the opportunity to sidle close to him. "Excuse me," she murmured. "I've been thinking over what you said yesterday, and I was hoping you could explain things better."

Dixie John looked startled. "I don't know what you're talking about."

Emma cocked her head, considering. Was he lying? No, she didn't think so. He had been trying to tell her something in the saloon, before Blackjack interrupted them. But clearly he didn't remember that now. "I was trying to find some answers about our trouble with the newspaper," she pressed. "And you told me . . ."

Something—panic?—flared in Dixie John's bloodshot eyes. He shifted his weight warily. "I don't know what you're going on about," he muttered. Then he turned and shoved out the door.

❧

"I want you to set type for me today," Mother told Emma as they left the boardinghouse that morning. "I did it for the prospectus because time was so short. But you need to learn."

"But I have some . . . some other things to do." Seeing Dixie John so nervous that morning had heightened Emma's suspicions, and she'd decided to pursue this bird's-eye idea further. Unfortunately, she'd have to do it by herself. Jeremy was needed at home today.

"You need to learn the newspaper business from the ground up. You'll never make a good editor and publisher if you don't know—"

"But I don't want to be an editor!" Emma knew she was fraying her mother's patience, but her own patience was frayed, too.

Mother stepped over a pile of ox droppings. "Emma Henderson! Don't you realize how lucky you are? I'm trying to teach you skills that will serve you for the rest of your life!"

Emma swallowed hard. "Mother," she said, in as docile a

tone as she could manage, "may I just go see Mr. Torkelson before I meet you at the newspaper office? I have one more question to ask him about the fire. For my article." Mother hesitated, then nodded. Emma veered in the direction she had taken the evening before when following The Whistler.

When The Whistler had disappeared into the darkness, he'd been near a few enterprises at the edge of town. One was a makeshift store of sorts in a big canvas tent, where a man sold merchandise left behind by "go-backers"— folks who had wearied of life in the goldfields or the frontier town and headed back east. Another was a three-sided shack where a huge German with a turnip-shaped nose hammered horseshoes and gate hinges on his portable forge. And beyond those were the cabin, stable, corral, and storage sheds where Mr. Torkelson operated his freight business. Emma wanted to start with him. He was friendly and wouldn't mind answering questions.

When Emma surveyed the commotion in the freight yard, she saw only Mr. Torkelson's sons unloading goods from a wagon train. No sign of a slight man with a limp. She found the wiry proprietor in the office with a customer. "Three cents a pound, firm," he was saying.

"Two and a half!"

Mr. Torkelson shook his head. "No, three. I got to transfer everything from the wagons to pack-jacks to get up to the mines, ya? Three cents!"

Emma waited until Mr. Torkelson was finished before approaching. "Excuse me. I have a question. Does a man with a limp work for you?"

Mr. Torkelson frowned, rubbing his chin. "Ya. Why? Hass he caused some trouble?"

Emma hesitated. What could she say that wouldn't sound ridiculous? "I heard him whistling my father's favorite song. It gave me a start. What's the man's name?"

"George Troxwell."

The name meant nothing to her. "Has he worked for you long?"

"Oh—joost a week or so. I needed an extra hand, and he iss good with the animals."

"Is he here now?" Emma's heart began to skitter.

But Mr. Torkelson shook his head. "He left early on a run. Won't be back till tonight, I don't think."

"Mr. Torkelson . . ." Emma hesitated. "Is Mr. Troxwell the hauler who was here the day of the fire? You said one of your men had been here just before the fire started."

Mr. Torkelson's eyes narrowed. "Ya. He iss the one. But he left before that paper burned."

I don't believe it, Emma thought, but since she had no proof, she couldn't speak her mind. Instead, she forced a smile. "I'll probably stop back later to meet Mr. Troxwell." She turned to go, then paused. "Oh—one more thing. Night before last, was Mr. Troxwell making a late delivery?"

Mr. Torkelson eyed her dubiously but reached for an

account book. He traced down a list of entries with a dirty finger. "Ya. Here it iss. He wass gone overnight, hauling a cookstove out to a ranch."

"Um, can you see if he was in town the two nights before that?"

Mr. Torkelson frowned again. "Ya. Joost that one night he was gone. But why—"

"Thank you!" Emma hurried into the morning sunshine before he could ask *her* questions. Nothing made sense yet, but she was making progress. The Whistler had appeared outside the Hendersons' window every night but one: the first night Emma had sat up to wait for him—the night Troxwell was gone on a freight run.

George Troxwell had to be The Whistler. But how did he know about Father's favorite song? And why was he taunting them with it? Why would he do such a hateful thing? This Troxwell must have set their paper shipment on fire, too—he'd had the perfect opportunity. Had he also stolen their press handle and dumped over the type-case? If not, who was he working with?

And what else did they have planned?

Emma's stomach turned over and her palms felt sweaty. George Troxwell had followed the Hendersons all the way from Chicago to this forlorn town in Colorado Territory. And that night, when he got back to Twin Pines, Emma intended to meet Mr. Troxwell and find out why.

CHAPTER 11
WITH A BIRD'S EYE

Mother kept Emma busy for the rest of the day. Emma learned how to position type sticks and measure margins and set type. She was ready to shriek with frustration by the time Mother released her. "You did well," Mother said. "You may run along now. It looks like the rain is ending, and Mrs. Sloane won't serve supper for an hour. I'll get a few more things done here."

Emma bolted for the door. Time was wasting, and she had some investigating to do!

Clouds scudded across the sky as she emerged from the print shack. *First stop: Mr. Spaulding's office,* she decided. She found the land office empty but the door unlocked. Hadn't Mr. Spaulding learned his lesson when their key was stolen? She stepped inside. Surely he wouldn't mind if she examined his map.

She stood before the bird's-eye map with her hands

clasped behind her back, studying again the slanted aerial view of the pretty town Mr. Spaulding had envisioned sprouting up among the foothills. If only she knew what she was looking for! She squinted at the tidy grid of streets, waiting for inspiration. Nothing came. What on earth—

"Emma? May I help you?" Mr. Spaulding's voice behind her was sharp. Emma almost jumped from her skin.

"Oh—Mr. Spaulding! I didn't hear you come in. I was just—ah—admiring your map. I hope you don't mind."

Mr. Spaulding walked to his desk and sat down. "I don't mind. But I do have business to attend to just now." He shuffled quickly through some papers, then sat back and regarded her. A drop of perspiration rolled down his forehead, and he rubbed it away impatiently.

"I beg your pardon," Emma sighed. She turned to go, then paused. She'd learned nothing from the bird's-eye map, but perhaps she could clear up another question. "Mr. Spaulding? I visited Tildy Pearce yesterday, and she mentioned that she'd never gotten her land deed. All she has is her receipt for the payment to you."

Mr. Spaulding frowned. "I must have tucked it away with my other papers by mistake. I'll take care of it."

"Excuse me, then," Emma murmured. She slipped back outside. Crackers! All she'd accomplished was annoying Mr. Spaulding. As to Dixie John's garbled advice—nothing! She pulled out her notebook and drew a heavy line through the words *Bird's-eye map?*

She glared at the second line: *The Raven?* The last thing she wanted to do was visit Blackjack's saloon again! But she had to try to unravel Dixie John's advice, crazy as it seemed. Stiffing up her spine, she marched down the boardwalk to the saloon and stepped inside.

The Raven smelled of tobacco and strong drink. Emma paused. The fiddler was nowhere in sight. A lively card game against the far wall was attracting the most attention. One young man in dirty miner's clothing sat hunched near a sputtering candle, reading a letter and wiping away homesick tears. The bartender plunked a glass and a spoon on the bar beside another miner, who crumbled soda crackers into the whiskey and began spooning the odd mixture into his mouth. "I promised my wife I wouldn't drink," he explained to Emma when he caught her staring.

Good glory. No wonder Miss Amaretta railed against drink! What was Emma doing here? Looking in the bird's eye? Thunderation! It was a fool's errand.

She was about to leave when Blackjack came down the staircase at the back of the room and saw her. "Why, Miss Emma!" he said, joining her. "What brings you back to The Raven? Come to solicit an advertisement to print in your newspaper, or to ask more questions?"

His smile didn't reach his eyes. A sudden thought stilled Emma's tongue. Had Blackjack interrupted Dixie John the day before to spare her a conversation with a drunkard—or had he done it to keep Dixie John from saying too much? If so, did he know that Emma was trying to figure out the meaning behind Dixie John's slurred words? Was Blackjack working with The Whistler?

She plastered a smile on her face. "I was looking for Tildy Pearce," she managed. That wasn't a complete lie. She needed to tell Tildy what she'd learned about the missing land deed.

"Tildy's not here. If she comes in this evening, shall I tell her to call at the boardinghouse?"

"Yes, please." Emma turned to leave with the distinct impression that Blackjack wanted her to go.

Outside, she sat down on the boardwalk to consider her options. Visiting The Raven hadn't helped her understand Dixie John's ramblings any more than studying Mr. Spaulding's map had. The only other idea she'd come up with involved climbing the twin pines behind the land office. "This is ridiculous!" she muttered. She wished she had a better idea. She wished she could talk things over with Jeremy. But she didn't, and she couldn't. Mr. Torkelson had said that George Troxwell—The Whistler—wouldn't be back until evening, so she had time on her hands. With an enormous sigh, she pushed to her feet.

The twin ponderosa pines towered behind Mr. Spaulding's land office. The shady ground beneath was littered with prickly pine cones. Emma put a hand on the tree's rough bark. It smelled of vanilla. Could she do this? *Climbs easy as a ladder,* Jeremy had said. Emma stared at the lower branches doubtfully. They were stumpy and dead, so she wouldn't have boughs and needles to climb through for the first few feet. But the branches most definitely were not spaced as evenly as rungs on a ladder. Emma wasn't even sure how to begin. How was she supposed to get her feet up to the lowest branch? It was at least waist-high.

Finally she wedged her right foot in the V where the two trunks separated. That gained her some height. She reached above her head, grasped a sturdy dead branch with both hands, and tried to position her left foot on the lowest branch. But her foot disappeared in the tent of her long petticoats and skirt.

"Oh!" she fumed, stepping back down. Drat Jeremy for working at home today! After looking carefully in both directions, she heaved her skirts above her left knee, exposing a white pantalette. With her left foot now free, she managed to lodge it on the branch and heave herself up.

There! She was actually climbing the tree! But three feet off the ground, she realized that she'd trapped herself. She'd reached a higher handhold, but when she tried to move her right foot higher, it too got tangled in her skirts. She couldn't let go without losing her balance, and she couldn't find a safe foothold for her right shoe.

She froze in the tree, stuck. A magpie landed on a branch above her head and began to scold. "Oh, hush!" Emma snapped. The skin on her palms began to ache. When she tried again to find the foothold she needed, her shoe landed on a fold of cotton and skidded off. She heard the sound of ripping cloth, and the branch slipped from her hands. Then she hit the ground. Hard.

Tears welled in her eyes, and for a moment she lay on the pine needles feeling sorry for herself. Her right arm and hip hurt where she'd landed on them, and she'd torn her dress. She missed Judith Littleton. Her mother neglected her. A saloon owner had threatened her, and a drunken Confederate had given her some nonsensical message. And a man she'd never even heard of was scaring her with a private song he had no business knowing about.

Finally she sat up and took stock, letting anger steam away her self-pity. She didn't seem to be seriously injured, and the dress could be mended. And—she would die of pure and absolute stubbornness before letting the stupid twin pines get the better of her.

When the solution crept into her mind, she nudged it away. But it slunk back, not to be ignored. "Oh, why not," Emma sighed. Everything else was turning upside down, wasn't it? She stood up, dusted herself off, and headed for the boardinghouse.

❧

Emma waited until Mother went back to the print shop after supper before putting her plan in action. Even then, she skulked at the boardinghouse door until a mule train had moved past with a snap of the muleskinner's whip, and the laundress marching down the street had disappeared into Mr. Boggs's store. For once, Emma was glad that the foothills were so often visited by late-afternoon storms. Lingering clouds and the evening's lengthening shadows provided at least the pretense of cover as she slid from the boardinghouse and dashed across the street. The skin between her shoulder blades itched, waiting for unknown boys to throw eggs. *Bloomers! Bloomers!* But no one hurled either taunts or eggs, and she plunged into the narrow alley between the land office and The Raven completely—she hoped—unnoticed.

She faced the twin pines with grim determination, stepped into the wedge between the trunks, and began to climb. It *still* wasn't as easy as Jeremy had promised. She had to snake between limbs that poked where her head needed to go, and the branches were not conveniently spaced for either hands or feet. But the trousers of her Reform Dress kept her from tripping.

She climbed about eight feet from the ground before pausing. She'd reached the needle-covered boughs and took a moment to savor that small victory. She slid onto a branch and rested, enjoying the scent of pine and the tiny sighs of the boughs swaying in the breeze. She glanced down at her dangling feet, clad in leather boots that emerged from her trousers. What if Judith could see her now? Or Miss Amaretta? Emma intended to sneak back to her bedroom to change before anyone was the wiser.

After a moment she glanced up and realized with a pang how far she was from the top. Crackers! How had Jeremy ever climbed high enough to see over the buildings? Should *she* try to climb that high?

No. Definitely not. Daylight was fading. She needed to get back to the boardinghouse, change clothes, and begin thinking about how to handle the confrontation with George Troxwell. In fact, it was time to enlist Mother's help. And Mule Tom's. She would surely feel better facing The Whistler with Mule Tom's reassuring bulk beside her.

But before she began to worm her way down, a sudden creak from below caught her attention. Craning her neck, she saw the back door of the land office inch open. Mr. Spaulding emerged. He tugged on his vest, looking in both directions, before shutting the door behind him.

Unnoticed, Emma felt a bit ashamed for spying—but she had no intention of calling attention to herself, up a tree in a Reform Dress! Through the branches she watched Mr. Spaulding slink against the land office wall, dart across the alley, and stop at the back door of The Raven—the door Emma had noticed leading into the saloon's private room. He knocked twice and slipped inside.

Emma shook her head. Oh, if only Miss Amaretta had seen that! The poor woman believed that she'd succeeded in convincing Mr. Spaulding to give up his

visits to The Raven. Instead, he was sneaking in the back
door! Mother had said Mr. Spaulding didn't have the sense
of a goose. Evidently he didn't have much of a conscience
either, if he could still look Miss Amaretta in the eye.

So what *was* the town founder doing in The Raven?
Drinking? Gambling? Curiosity pricked at Emma as she
carefully climbed to the ground. She crept along the land
office and saloon walls, then crouched beneath the private
room's window. The paisley curtains were drawn but the
window was ajar, and Blackjack's voice—for once not oiled
smooth—carried outside. "Spaulding, you're a fool. Why
are you back here?"

"You *can't* turn me away!" Emma pictured Spaulding
mopping his forehead. "Nothing is working out as I had
planned. I *will* pay my debts, but you have to give me a
chance—"

Emma heard Blackjack interrupt to greet several men
who had apparently just entered the room. Then she heard
the click of the interior door being closed.

You have no business listening to this, Emma scolded herself. Still, she couldn't bring herself to creep away. No
wonder Mr. Spaulding was so panicked about the town
failing, if he had gambling debts to worry about, too!

"Ah, we're all here. Fill your glasses, gentlemen, so
we can get started." That was Blackjack again. Evidently
he wasn't going to turn Mr. Spaulding away. After a few
moments of mumbled conversation, Emma heard the

scrape of chairs. Then Blackjack spoke again, easy as ever. "The ace of hearts, gentlemen, is the winning card. The ace of hearts. Who feels lucky?"

A sliver of lamplight showed where the curtains didn't quite meet. Emma eased to her feet and dared a peek. She could just make out a slice of the table, a man's hand holding a fan of cards—

Emma heard the tiniest whisper of sound behind her, but too late. A strong hand clamped over her mouth just as an arm circled her belly and jerked her back against her attacker's chest. Her heart thumped in panic. *Let me go!* she tried to scream. Her arms were pinned at her sides, but she kicked wildly. As her heel met her attacker's shinbone, he loosened his grip just enough to let her twist in his grasp.

The shadows and his low felt hat almost hid his face, but Emma saw narrow eyes, then a mouth twisted into a hideous grin. She tried again to scream but heard only a pounding in her ears as the man clamped harder across her mouth and nose. She felt herself being dragged deeper into the shadows, away from the saloon wall. Then everything faded to black.

CHAPTER 12

THE WHISTLER'S STORY

The light hurt Emma's eyes and she closed them again. Where was she? Lying on her back ... in a pile of straw, by the feel of it. The close air smelled of manure. A stable. Someone had grabbed her and dragged her to a stable. At least she didn't seem to be hurt, aside from the hip and arm she'd bruised when she fell from the twin pines. Screwing up all of her courage, she cracked her eyes open again.

The bright spot of light came from a lantern set on the wooden floor in a spot scraped free of straw. The blackness beyond sorted itself into shapes and shadows as Emma's eyes adjusted. She was in a horse stall. A man sat against the stall wall, hugging his knees. Emma's bones grew cold as she remembered being grabbed—and her attacker's horrible, leering grin.

But now the man stared at the floor, not at her. Could she slip past him? Probably not. This man had trailed her and Mother all the way from Chicago—heaven only knew what he'd do if she tried to escape.

Emma swallowed a whimper. *Just run!* a voice in her head urged. But her legs quivered like custard. The best she could manage was sitting up.

The man tugged his shapeless felt hat lower on his forehead so that his face remained shadowed. Then he sat up straighter against the wall. "You're not hurt," he said.

"W—what do you want?" Emma quavered.

"You're not hurt," he repeated.

Emma rubbed her arms, confusion mingling with her fear. She heard a munching sound, the stamp of a hoof. Was this Mr. Torkelson's stable? Oh, please, let it be!

She licked her lips and dared another question. "Are you George Troxwell?"

He jerked his head up in surprise, and Emma saw again his horrible, twisted sneer. Fear danced damp and cold over her skin. Then she realized that his grimace was actually a scar—a jagged scar that pulled at the right side of his mouth and burned across his cheek. "I'm George," he mumbled.

Emma drew a deep breath. "Why did you grab me?"

"They might have hurt you."

"*You* hurt me! And you—"

"Those were bad men!"

Emma rubbed her head, which was beginning to ache. "Bad men . . . you mean in the saloon? The men playing cards in that back room?"

Troxwell nodded. "They wouldn't like you sneaking around. They're bad men."

"Bad—how?"

"They gamble. Gamblers get angry when they lose. I didn't want them to get angry at you."

Nothing made sense. "You were trying to *save* me from trouble?"

He looked confused. "Yes! I've been guarding you. You and your mother."

"*Guarding* us! But—" She broke off and cocked her head. Someone outside was bellowing her name.

"Emma Henderson!"

"In here!" she yelled, lurching to her feet. When Mule Tom materialized from the darkness, Emma wanted to weep with relief.

He planted himself in the narrow stall opening. "Miss Emma! Oh, thank the Lord! What you doin' here? You all right, child?"

"I—I think so." The weight of Mule Tom's hand on her shoulder steadied her.

"We been worried sick!" He glared at Troxwell. "What you doin' with Miss Emma?"

"I didn't hurt her!"

"Miss Emma?" Mule Tom asked, his steel gaze never leaving the other man.

"He—he grabbed me when I was—well, eavesdropping." Emma was still trying to sort out everything that had happened. "But Mule Tom, I think this is the man who—"

"Miss Emma, your mama needs to hear whatever you got to say. I promised her I'd bring you back to the boardinghouse if I found you." Mule Tom pointed a big finger at George Troxwell. "You, too. Let's go."

⚬

Ten minutes later, Emma endured her mother's tearful embrace and simultaneous tongue-lashing in Mrs. Sloane's parlor. "Do you have *any* idea how I felt when I got back tonight and found you gone? What *were* you thinking?"

Mrs. Sloane appeared with a pot of hot tea, looking curious, then disappeared. Mule Tom and George Troxwell perched awkwardly on the edge of two parlor chairs. Before Mother finished, Mrs. Sloane ushered Tildy Pearce into the room. Crackers! Emma had forgotten about asking Blackjack to have Tildy call this evening. Wide-eyed, Tildy backed into a corner. Mrs. Sloane gave in to curiosity and settled down, too.

Finally Mother paused for breath, and Emma seized the opening. "Mother, please listen for a minute. I have to explain some things. I've been hearing a man whistle *Maggie by My Side* at night here in Twin Pines, just like we did in Chicago—"

"What?" Mother gasped.

"You were always asleep, or gone," Emma explained.

"At first I was afraid you'd tell me I was dreaming. And then . . . well, you were already so worried . . . I didn't want to add to your burden. But I think this is the man who's been doing it." She nodded at George Troxwell.

Mother's eyes widened as she turned on Troxwell. "*Why?* Why did you want to frighten us? And how did you know about that song?"

George twisted his hat in his hands. "But—but I didn't want to scare you! It was to make you feel safe! Captain Henderson always said you loved that song."

Mother's hand flew to her mouth. "Captain Henderson?" she faltered. "You knew my husband?"

"Of course," Troxwell said patiently. "He was my captain. In the war. He whistled that song when he was sad. It made him feel better."

This man had been with her father during his last years! And that scar . . . had it been a rifle ball? Or a cannon shot? Emma shuddered.

"What is your name?" Mother asked.

"George, ma'am. George Troxwell."

Recognition slid over Mother's face. "You're the man who wrote me the letter. After my husband died."

"Yes, ma'am. I was with him. Before he died he asked me, 'Will you see to my wife and daughter?' I promised him I would. I promised him!" Tears welled in his eyes. A lump rose in Emma's throat.

"Then I got wounded, and I couldn't write you for a

while," George Troxwell continued. "But I didn't forget!
It would have been my honor to marry you, ma'am. But you
didn't want that. I didn't know what to do, except try to
keep watch over you and Miss Emma. I was in a hospital
for a long time after the war ended. Then I had to find work
and save enough money to come find you—"

"So it really was just coincidence that we first heard
you whistling the night Mother got Mr. Spaulding's letter,"
Emma blurted.

"And you followed us all the way from Chicago,"
Mother murmured. "Merciful heaven."

For a moment no one spoke. Mrs. Sloane dabbed at
her eyes with her handkerchief. A moth fluttered against
the oil lamp burning on a corner table.

Then Emma remembered. "But why did you want the
newspaper to fail? I mean . . ." She felt her cheeks flush.
"It was you, wasn't it? Who stole the press lever, and burned
the paper, and—"

"No!" George shook his head. "I don't know anything
about that! I wouldn't do *anything* to hurt you ladies!" He
looked at Mother. "You got to believe me! I promised the
captain!"

Mother put a calming hand on his arm. "We *do* believe
you, Mr. Troxwell. I know my husband—" Her voice
shook, and she took a deep breath to steady it. "I know
he would be most grateful for your concern. As I am."
She cocked her head, considering. "It's getting very late,

but I'd like to talk with you again. Where are you staying?"

"I work for Nels Torkelson. He lets me sleep in the stable."

"May Emma and I visit you?"

George agreed and took his leave, looking relieved to escape the parlor. Mrs. Sloane disappeared, and Mule Tom left, too. Mother narrowed her eyes at Emma. "You should have *told* me about—"

"Excuse me, Mother, but I need to introduce Tildy." Emma gratefully turned to Tildy, who looked bewildered by the evening's events. "She's the one I told you about. Her husband ran off and left her. She's been walking to town and dancing with the men at the saloon to earn money for a newspaper subscription."

"Merciful heaven!" Mother said again. She summoned an exhausted smile for Tildy. "Then it is indeed a pleasure to meet you."

"I'm ever so excited about the newspaper," Tildy said. "But I didn't mean to poke in on a family time." She turned to Emma. "Blackjack said you were looking for me?"

"I wanted to let you know about your land deed. Mother said you should have one. When I asked Mr. Spaulding, he said he just forgot to give it to you."

"Well, that explains it." Tildy nodded. "But I don't think I'll hound him about it for a day or two. He had a bad night, I think."

"Why do you say that?" Emma asked.

Tildy's face flushed in the lamplight. "Oh, it's none of my business, I guess. But I was taking a rest tonight, sitting back in the corner by that private room—I do that, sometimes, when my feet start to ache—and through the door I heard Blackjack and Mr. Spaulding get in a terrible row. That room's where the high-stakes games are, and it sounded like Mr. Spaulding lost tonight. Real quick and real bad. Mr. Spaulding wanted to keep going on credit, and Blackjack wouldn't give it to him."

"If this town survives, it will be in spite of Mr. Spaulding, not because of him," Mother murmured. But she was staring out the window, clearly thinking more about personal events than Mr. Spaulding's ever-growing list of faults.

After Tildy left, Mother blew out the lamp and put her arm around Emma's shoulders as they walked toward the stairs. "Well, it's been a night for surprises," she said. "Not the least of which is seeing you in your Reform Dress."

Emma stared at her legs. Thunderation! So much for changing into her dress before anyone saw her. Emma decided to change the subject before Mother had a chance to ask why Emma was wearing the Reform Dress. She wasn't ready to describe her ridiculous quest to "look with a bird's eye."

"What do you think of Mr. Troxwell?" she asked instead. "How strange, to follow us all the way to Colorado—whistling!"

"He was clearly devoted to your father. I think we

also need to remember that Mr. Troxwell obviously received a severe head wound. That, on top of seeing your father killed ... well, he may be ... not quite ... the whole man he was before the war." Mother shook her head. "I do believe he meant well, though. And oh, Emma! Think of the stories he can tell us about your father!"

Yes, that part would be wonderful. At the moment, though, all Emma could think of was a good night's sleep, uninterrupted by whistling in the dark. But just as the two of them started up the staircase, someone knocked lightly on the front door. Then Mule Tom stepped inside.

"Miz Henderson, I'm real sorry," he said, "but there's more trouble at the print shop."

᠆ᡏ

The lantern in Mule Tom's hand cast a glow on the mess. Emma clenched her fists. The precious ink keg had been dumped over, spilling a black pool into the sawdust. Pencils and coffee cups lay on the floor. A crease-pressing bone had been snapped in two. A few copies of the prospectus had been crumpled and tossed aside. Several articles Mother had written, left waiting to be set in type, had been torn to bits. Scrawled across one sheet in dark pencil were two words:

GO HOME!

"I must have left the door unlocked when I set out to look for Miss Emma," Mule Tom said in a low tone. "I'm more sorry than I can tell, Miz Henderson."

"It's not your fault," Mother said woodenly. "You found my daughter. That's all that really matters."

Emma felt a weight of guilt settle on her shoulders. Then her gaze picked out something in the rubble, almost hidden beneath the tin coffeepot. "Oh, no!" she breathed, crouching to examine the damage. Her mother's daguerreotype of Captain Henderson lay facedown on the floor. When Emma eased the case up, she saw that the glass image had shattered.

❧

The next morning, Mother, Mule Tom, and Emma began the cleanup. Emma tried not to remember the sight of her father's image in jagged shards. Who could be so cruel? What else would happen if the Hendersons *didn't* give up? But if they did quit . . . what then? They had no money. Would they live in a tent and take in miners' filthy laundry to survive?

For a while they worked in silence. We *have* to make *The Herald* succeed, Emma finally concluded, because we don't have any other choice. She paused from scraping ink-soaked sawdust into a pile. "Mother . . . Mr. Abbott's brother needs our first edition by Monday morning, or he'll have to leave for Indiana without it. And tomorrow is Sunday. Do you think we can still get the newspaper out in time?"

"I honestly don't know," Mother sighed. "Our new paper shipment is due tonight. But my articles . . ." She gestured at the scraps of paper.

"You can write them again," Emma dared. "I know you can."

"Well . . . probably. But we lost our ink. Although I suppose I could improvise some, if we can scare up enough lampblack and oil. And perhaps the Lord would understand if just this once we went to work after Sunday school tomorrow." She hesitated. "Mule Tom, what do you think? Are you willing to stick it out?"

"Yes, ma'am." He nodded calmly.

Mother chewed her lower lip. "I must say, this has unnerved me. And I am so disappointed with Mr. Spaulding that I'm starting not to care whether he gets his newspaper or not."

"But we're not just doing this for him!" Emma protested. "We're doing this for Jeremy's family, and Tildy Pearce, and—and everybody else who's counting on us."

Mother mustered a smile. "You remind me of your father sometimes, Emma. Yes, you're right. And you and I can't afford to give up anyway. I'll talk to the men on the Safety Committee. Maybe they can help keep an eye on things for us."

When Jeremy arrived, he and Mule Tom headed out to scrounge the ink supplies. By the time noon approached, the print shop was tidy and Mother was already rewriting one of her articles. "Shall I fetch you some dinner, Mother?" Emma asked.

"What? Is it so late?" Mother rubbed the fingers of her writing hand absently. "I'm not hungry. You go on. I want to get this down while it's still in my head."

Dinner at the boardinghouse included stewed gooseberries and sputtering-hot squabs served on rice, an adequate meal unfortunately marred by the addition of heavy, sour biscuits. Neither Dixie John nor Blackjack appeared. Miss Amaretta passed the meal in conversation with a young wife who'd just arrived in Twin Pines and was resting over a day before traveling on to the goldfields to meet her husband.

Emma toyed with her food, twisting her mind around her problems. The whistling business had been sorted out, but she still had no idea who was trying so hard to keep *The Twin Pines Herald* from being published. If Blackjack or Dixie John was behind it, she didn't know why, or how to prove it. She pulled out her notebook and opened it discreetly on her lap. She read over her notes. Only one suspect hadn't been questioned.

"And I've heard," Miss Amaretta advised the miner's wife, "that if you sit out in the evening, you ought to start little fires of pine needles in frying pans and set several of them about. The smoke keeps mosquitoes away."

The other woman nodded earnestly. "I do appreciate the advice."

Emma watched the exchange, considering her final suspect. Was it possible that Miss Amaretta was so opposed to Mother's Reform Dress ideas that she'd try to shut the paper down? Emma simply couldn't believe it. Besides, the press handle had been stolen before Miss Amaretta ever saw Mother wearing her Reform Dress. Still . . . asking a few good reporter questions couldn't do any harm. Emma didn't know what else to do.

Mrs. Sloane began to clear the dishes, and the miner's wife headed off to Mr. Boggs's store. Emma cleared her throat. "Miss Amaretta, may we talk for a few minutes?"

"Why, of course, dear! Come up to my room." Miss Amaretta led the way, holding her pale green skirt high enough to keep from tripping without showing so much as an ankle. It was an art Emma couldn't help admiring.

Miss Amaretta had managed to turn Mrs. Sloane's bare-bones room into a gracious retreat. Crocheted doilies covered the bureau and table, and lace curtains framed the windows. A pot of sprawling ivy stood in a wicker stand in the corner. Paintings of sweet-faced children and vases of flowers graced the walls.

"Oh!" A wave of homesickness drenched Emma. She stopped in front of one of the paintings. "Did you do this?"

"Oh, no. I'm no artist. I had it carted out from home."

"I like to paint," Emma admitted shyly. "I was learning about still lifes before we moved here."

Miss Amaretta smiled. "If you'd like to pick some flowers and arrange them in here to paint, you're welcome any time. Although I should think you'd rather paint flowers in the meadows, where God put them. I can't think of anything lovelier."

"Your room is lovely!"

"I suppose I've indulged myself, bringing so many things out from the East. But I like to feel at home." Miss Amaretta settled into one of the chairs in a small sitting area. "I hope to rent a little house one day, when I can afford it. I do fancy a true home."

"Mr. Spaulding was supposed to provide a house for Mother and me," Emma said, settling in the other chair. "It would be nice to have my own room again. And a kitchen."

"Gracious, yes!" Miss Amaretta lowered her voice. "Mrs. Sloane is an admirable housekeeper. But her cooking! Once, soon after I arrived, she made a cake and mistook cayenne pepper for ginger! One of the guests didn't stop coughing for ten minutes."

"And her biscuits are horrible!" Emma whispered, remembering Mrs. Littleton's buttermilk and soda biscuits: a good three inches high, crisp on the bottom and fluffy in the middle.

Miss Amaretta put a kind hand on Emma's arm.

"I'm sorry life brought you to Twin Pines. I imagine you'd rather be back east, with your friends."

Emma *would* rather be back east . . . but saying so seemed disloyal to Mother, and to her new friends—like Jeremy and Tildy—too. She jumped to her feet and prowled the room like a restless cat. She paused in front of Miss Amaretta's bureau, admiring the intricate silver inlay on her brush and comb. Then she noticed the mirror hanging above the bureau, and she caught her breath. The oval of reflective glass was encased in a heavy wooden frame. The wood was swirled with the same pattern she'd admired years ago, in her father's safebox. Emma touched the wood with a gentle finger, hearing again her father's laugh. She blinked several times, hard.

"Emma?" Miss Amaretta appeared in the mirror behind her, looking concerned.

Emma tried to smile. "I was just . . . just admiring this. My father had a box made of this same kind of swirly wood."

"It's lovely, isn't it? It's bird's-eye maple. I brought this from Ohio— Emma? Emma!"

"Excuse me!" Emma shouted, bolting for the door.

CHAPTER 13

THE BOX

Showing far more than an ankle, Emma skidded into her own room and slammed the door. Sprawling belly-down on her bed, she opened her notebook to a clean page. On the left side she listed all the attacks made on the newspaper. Then, digging back through her memory, she started another list opposite the first:

Press lever stolen	*Mr. Spaulding knew when we were coming and unpacked the press himself.*
Paper shipment burned	*I told Mr. Sp. that Mr. Torkelson expected the shipment that day.*
Typecase dumped over	*Mr. Sp. had the key to the print shop (which he said was stolen).*

Ink spilled and articles
destroyed

Mr. Sp. had time after losing
the poker game to go by the
print shop while Mule Tom
was looking for me. Maybe
angry about losing the game?

What else? Mr. Spaulding had seemed annoyed to find Emma studying his map, and had looked through his papers nervously before addressing her. He had gambling debts. *Gamblers get angry when they lose,* Mr. Troxwell had said. *A man in debt is a desperate man,* Tildy had said.

Emma chewed her pencil. She couldn't imagine why Mr. Spaulding would bring her and Mother all the way to Twin Pines, then try to drive them away. But she did have a good idea where to look for the answer. "Look in the bird's eye—" Dixie John had mumbled, before Blackjack interrupted him. That part, at least, finally made sense. Bird's-eye *box.* If Mr. Spaulding was hiding secrets, they were no doubt locked in his storage box made of bird's-eye maple.

Emma rolled on her back and stared at the ceiling. How was Dixie John involved? What connection could a Confederate veteran have with a land speculator from New York? She tried to recall what she'd heard about Dixie John. He periodically headed into the hills, Jeremy had said, hoping to strike it rich in the goldfields. When his luck ran out, he drifted back to Twin Pines and looked

for odd jobs. He'd been known to chop wood for gold-
field widows, or dig wells—

"Oh!" Emma sat up. She considered a moment,
then darted from the bedroom and thundered down
the steps. She found Mrs. Sloane in the kitchen, cutting
up a dead rabbit for stew meat. "Mrs. Sloane, may I ask
you something? Do you own this place?"

Mrs. Sloane frowned. "I most surely do, if it's any
business of yours. When my husband died, he left me
enough to buy this plot and have the house built."

"Has Mr. Spaulding ever offered to buy the land
back from you?"

Mrs. Sloane snorted. "Now, why would he do that?
He's got enough money troubles, from what I hear, to—
Child? Where are you going?"

Within an hour, Emma had learned that most of
the businesspeople in town still rented their lots from
Mr. Spaulding. A few had purchased the land, but
Mr. Spaulding hadn't offered to buy any of *their* land
back—just the Abbotts' land, south of Tildy Pearce's
farm. According to Jeremy, Mr. Spaulding had also
bought back the farm north of Tildy's place. And the
Pearces had paid Mr. Spaulding for the middle farm
but had never received a deed to their land.

Emma was breathless by the time she plunged into
the print shack. Mule Tom and Jeremy were busy con-
cocting ink in a copper kettle, but Mother gave her a

stern frown. "Emma Catherine Henderson! Didn't I scold you just last night for disappearing without letting me know where you were going?"

"Yes, but wait." Emma held up a hand. "I have some news for you."

༄

It was a dubious posse that confronted Mr. Spaulding in his office later that afternoon: Emma, Mother, Mule Tom, Jeremy, Mr. Abbott, and Mr. Boggs, who had closed his store to join them. They had discussed sending someone to Denver City or Golden for a sheriff, but they'd discarded that plan. "We can't prove anything," Jeremy's father pointed out. "All we can do is challenge the man, bluff if we have to, and hope he crumbles." As the group filed into a semicircle in front of Mr. Spaulding's desk, Emma hoped Mr. Spaulding would crumble quickly. The whole business was twisting her stomach like laundry through a wringer.

Mr. Spaulding stood up. "What's all this?"

"We have concerns to discuss with you," Mother said crisply, and spelled out what Emma had pieced together.

Mr. Spaulding began shaking his head before she'd finished. "That's absurd," he sputtered. "Preposterous! I've put my lifeblood into this town, and it needs a newspaper! I *hired* you, for God's sake—although I see now that I made a terrible mistake. This is what comes of hiring women, I suppose."

Emma decided to charge in before Mother exploded. "We don't know what this is all about," she admitted. "But we think it has something to do with these properties." She walked to the big map and pointed to the three farms north of town, along the creek. "This near one is the Abbotts', and you tried to buy their land back. This far one you *did* buy back. And this one in the middle is where Tildy Pearce and her husband settled. You took their money, but you never gave them the legal deed to the land."

Mr. Spaulding's face paled, and he began fishing in a pocket—undoubtedly for the ever-present handkerchief. "I told you, I merely forgot—"

"What about my land?" Mr. Abbott interrupted. "Why did you try to buy me out? Why the farm families in Peaceful Valley, but not anyone in town?"

Sweat began to dribble down the land agent's forehead. Emma watched with fascination as dark, damp patches appeared on the front of his shirt as well. He fumbled in another pocket.

"Oh, for heaven's sake, here!" Mother slapped her own handkerchief down in front of him, then pointed at the storage box. "We think we can find the answers we're looking for in that box."

Mopping his face, Spaulding dropped into his chair. "My private papers—I haven't—you can't—"

"Oh, yes, we can!" Mr. Boggs erupted. The short, bald storekeeper was shaking with fury. "I poured my life's savings into my store, and into this town! If you're dealing shady business, you're going to come clean *right now!*" He took a deep breath, straightening his cravat. "Now. We can do this one of three ways. One: You can open that box for us. Two: This man—" he nodded at Mule Tom, standing silent and huge at the end of the row—"can smash it open with his fist. Three: We can all sit here quietly and wait for the Safety Committee members we sent to fetch a sheriff. It's up to you. But we *will* see what you've got in there."

For one horrible moment, Emma thought Mr. Spaulding was going to burst into tears. Finally he shoved the box toward them with shaking hands. After a moment of fumbling in his pocket, he pushed the key after it. "There. There! Are you satisfied now? You've ruined me!" With elbows planted on the desk, he buried his face in his hands.

Mr. Boggs worked the key and lifted the lid. Mother and Mr. Abbott leaned close as the storekeeper began passing papers around.

"Here's the deed to Tildy's farm," Mr. Abbott said grimly. "Only it isn't made out to the Pearces. It's made out to James Spaulding."

Mother squinted at what appeared to be a letter. "Listen to this. 'I regret that I cannot immediately

commence the trip you propose. I am under contract
with the Lost Eagle Mining Company until the end of
July. At that time, I shall travel to Twin Pines to survey the
river land you described.' The letter is signed 'Professor
J. B. Swallow, Mineralogist.'"

"Hey, I know him!" Jeremy exclaimed. "He came
through here once before. He took me rock hunting.
He knows a lot about rocks and minerals."

"Especially gold, perhaps?" Jeremy's father reached
into the box and extracted a lumpy felt pouch. After peer-
ing inside, he upended it over the table. Emma gasped as
half a dozen golden nuggets—one almost as big as a hen's
egg—tumbled out.

Jeremy grabbed one and examined it. "It's not pyrite—
fool's gold. It's real," he said. "Where did you get these,
Mr. Spaulding? Professor Swallow said there likely wasn't
any gold around Twin Pines, beyond the dust in the creek.
And that's not worth the time it takes to pan it out."

"I think I know," Emma said. "Those nuggets came
out of the well on Tildy Pearce's farm—right? You hired
Dixie John to dig a well on that land before you sold it."

Mother nodded. "You no doubt hoped a well would
help attract a buyer."

"And Dixie John found the nuggets when he was
digging the well!" Emma folded her arms. "That's why the
well was never finished. Tildy said the well on her place
was only half dug."

"What did you do then, bribe Dixie John to keep quiet?" Mr. Abbott's voice was cold as January. "So you could buy the rest of us out cheap?"

"I *had* to!" Mr. Spaulding's red-rimmed eyes pleaded for sympathy. "Don't you see? I'm in debt! I owe *thousands* of dollars—"

"To who?" Mr. Abbott snapped impatiently.

"To Blackjack," Emma said. "Am I right?"

"I don't know how it happened," Mr. Spaulding quavered. "Just a few friendly poker games . . . and then I had to wager more, to earn back what I'd lost . . . I've *never* had such bad luck before. That's all it was, bad luck!"

"Blackjack began pressuring you for the money," Mother guessed. "Then—then you stumbled onto a gold strike. So you tried to cheat the Abbotts and their neighbors off their land, before they found out about the nuggets. But . . . why attack the newspaper? Why bring me and Emma all the way out here, just to scare us back to Chicago?"

"It wasn't personal! Don't you see?" Mr. Spaulding begged. "I could have paid Blackjack easily if Twin Pines had developed as planned. But it didn't. Once I knew about the gold, the best I could hope for was that everyone would get discouraged and move away. It's happened in dozens of towns all over the territory. Then I could have mined the gold quietly, and no one would have been the wiser! But everyone was *hammering* me to hire a publisher. I put it off as long as I could. Finally, when

I got your letter, I thought I was safe. I thought, if I just hire a woman . . ." His voice trailed away—probably silenced, Emma thought, by the sparks flying from Mother's eyes.

Those eyes narrowed to slits. "You thought that if you hired a woman, the paper would never see its first edition. Is that it?"

Mr. Spaulding wilted before her gaze. He planted his face back in his sweaty palms.

"Spaulding!" Mr. Boggs snapped. He waited until the other man looked at him. "This is how it's going to be. We are keeping the nuggets, the letter, and the deed until a sheriff arrives. You may own Tildy Pearce's farm on paper, but we don't think a judge will see it that way. As for your gambling debt, well, if you don't get carted off to jail for cheating the Pearces and terrorizing the Hendersons—and I hope to God that you do—then it's up to Blackjack. But until the authorities arrive, members of the Safety Committee will see that you don't leave this building. Is that understood?"

Spaulding nodded. He looked dazed.

Mother sailed from the room, and the others followed. Emma lingered to take one last look at the man who had caused so much trouble. "I'm not a bad man," he whispered, and nodded at the beautiful bird's-eye map of his dream. "I truly wanted that."

Emma struggled to find appropriate words. "Excuse

me," she said finally, crisp and cool. "I have a newspaper
to help publish."

⚔

On Monday morning, when Mr. Abbott drove his
wagon to the print shop at half past eleven, the Hendersons,
Mule Tom, and Jeremy were waiting outside.

"This is my brother Sam," Jeremy's father said, intro-
ducing the man who rode with him.

"Sorry I haven't had the chance to make your acquaintance sooner," Sam Abbott said. "I've been busy looking
over the lay of the land around here."

"How do you like what you've seen so far?" Mother
asked. She held a cup of coffee in her hands and squinted
as she looked into the sun—or maybe it was just the puffy,
dark rings beneath her eyes that made it appear that way.

"I like it well. Real well. That's what I'm fixing to tell
the people waiting for my report."

"Well, we have something to send along with you,"
Mother told him. If Emma hadn't been so tired, she would
have danced a jig as she watched Mule Tom disappear into
the print shack, then reappear a moment later with an
armful of crisp, neatly folded newspapers.

"It's finished." A broad smile spread across Jeremy's
father's face. *"The Twin Pines Herald."* He picked up one of
the newspapers and looked it over—the headline banners,

the news articles, the editorials and advertisements, even the children's news and ladies' advice column. He nodded at Jeremy, who beamed.

Sam Abbott smiled, too. "These look fine, ma'am. I'm sure the folks back home will be pleased to get them. I'm obliged."

"Our pleasure."

Jeremy scrambled into the wagon, and the others watched the Abbotts rumble back toward the main street to wait for the stagecoach. No one moved. "I'm going to bed," Emma said finally. Her eyes felt sandy and her muscles ached. She'd never stayed up all night before. But after only a few plodding steps, she turned around. "Hey, Mother? Mule Tom?" Her face stretched into a smile. "We did it."

Mother pushed a straggle of loose hair from her face. "Yes, indeed," she said softly. "We did it."

Chapter 14
Surprises

Emma walked into the print shop, glad to escape the August sun. Mother was looking over trim lines of type in the press. "Good job, Tildy!" she exclaimed a moment later.

Tildy flushed. "Thank you, Miz Henderson. I tried ever so hard."

"I knew that anyone who spends her evenings reading a spelling book would make an excellent typesetter," Mother said. "All right, Mr. Troxwell. You can ink the type now."

"Mother!" Emma said.

Mother looked up and blinked. "Oh, Emma! How long have you been standing there?"

"Long enough," Emma said, but she smiled.

Mother nodded at Emma's attire. "You must be going riding with Jeremy. That's about the only time I see you in your Reform Dress."

"I usually don't need bloomers to help out around the

print shop," Emma protested. "And we agreed—"

"I know, I know." Mother waved a hand. "It's your choice— Oh, Mrs. Carter! Did you come by to discuss an advertisement? I understand you're selling pies . . ."

Emma stepped over to say hello to Tildy, who was wearing her own Reform Dress. "How do you like your new job?"

"It's wonderful! I never thought I'd be helping print a newspaper!" A look of awe slipped over her face.

Emma knew that Mother was happy to have Tildy, and Mr. Troxwell, too—especially since Mule Tom had headed back to the goldfields. Still, Emma couldn't help putting a sympathetic hand on her friend's arm. "I heard about Professor Swallow's report. I'm sorry. I wish there really *had* been a rich gold vein running through your land, instead of just those few nuggets."

Tildy shrugged. "Emma, it really doesn't matter."

"Good." Emma squeezed Tildy's hand, then turned to watch Mr. Troxwell inking the rows of type Tildy had positioned, his scarred face set with concentration. "How are you?" Emma asked, when he paused.

"Real good, Miss Emma," he said. "But I got to finish this job now."

"Then I won't keep you. I think that's Jeremy, anyway." Emma waved and hurried outside.

Jeremy was riding a gray mare named Cloud. "Mind riding two-fer-one?" he asked. "Pa needed the other horses today." He held his left foot free of the stirrup so that Emma could step up and swing behind the saddle.

Emma centered herself on the mare's broad rump. Jeremy had been giving her riding lessons all summer. She had abandoned the idea of riding sidesaddle the first time she lost her balance and promptly slid to the ground. "You'd have better balance if you rode astride," Jeremy had pointed out. "And since you've got that skirt-and-trousers getup . . ." Emma had given in, and she'd learned to love the freedom of pounding through the valley on horseback.

As Jeremy turned the mare north, Emma grabbed his arm. "Crackers! I forgot my hat. Can we stop back at the boardinghouse?"

"Sure." He paused to let a bullwhacker pass. "You know, I'm surprised you and your mother still live at Mrs. Sloane's after—what, more than two months?"

"I've got a plan about that." Emma lowered her voice. "Miss Amaretta wants a house, with a kitchen she can cook in, but she can't afford it. My mother can't afford it yet, either, but most of all she doesn't want to have to cook or keep a house tidy. So I'm figuring—"

Jeremy hooted. "Your mother and Miss Amaretta sharing a house?"

"No, really! They argue from habit more than anything else these days."

"It could work, I guess." Jeremy reined the horse

to a stop in front of the boardinghouse. "Hey, I've been meaning to ask you. Remember that rock I gave you? Did you ever bust it open?"

Emma flushed. "Well . . . actually . . . no."

Jeremy snorted. "We're going to do that right now," he announced. "Or no ride."

Emma crossed her fingers as she hurried up the stairs. She *thought* she had tucked the silly thing into the top dresser drawer. Yes—thank goodness, there it was. She examined the lumpy gray stone. She still thought it was as ugly as Twin Pines!

Rock in hand and straw hat in place, Emma let Jeremy take her around to the forge. The blacksmith was replacing the iron rim on a farmer's wagon wheel—an operation that involved a fire pit, glowing iron, brute force, and a clear sense of timing—so Emma and Jeremy slid to the ground and waited in the shade beside his shack.

"You think your ma'll still need me, now that she's hired Tildy and George?" Jeremy asked. "Pa said I could help with the newspaper sometimes, even after that new teacher gets here and school starts."

Emma rolled her eyes. "Aren't you tired of it yet?"

"No! I think it's fun."

"Well . . . I suppose investigating a big story can be exciting."

"Like Mr. Spaulding causing so much trouble!"

Emma shook her head. She hadn't seen the land agent

since the sheriff had taken him off to Golden, the territorial capital. Spaulding was still in jail. "Yes. But mostly it's boring. I don't want to spend my life setting type, or even writing articles."

"So what *do* you want?"

Emma looked down the street, picturing the lush valley beyond Twin Pines. Asters and gentians were blooming now, and Jeremy promised that soon the aspen trees would turn as gold as candles. "Art is what I really like."

"Did you ever think about doing engravings for the newspaper? You know, those fancy illustrations they have in the big papers back east?"

"I don't know exactly how they do it. It's complicated, I think." Emma slapped at a mosquito, considering. "An artist makes the sketch, and then it gets copied onto a block of wood, and then someone has to carve away everything but the lines."

"I'm pretty good with a jackknife, and a chisel, too."

"Do you really think we could?" Emma felt a warm smile bubble slowly up from inside. "Well . . . crackers! Let's give it a try!"

"We'll start with something simple. Maybe a nice title block for the newspaper. What do you call those?"

"A masthead." Emma nodded, picturing the words "The Twin Pines Herald" in fancy letters, perhaps with a mountain range sketched in the background.

Jeremy looked at her sideways. "You know, when you

got here, I didn't figure you'd last long. I pegged you as a
go-backer for sure."

"I might have been, if Mother could have afforded to
buy tickets home," Emma admitted. She thought that over,
waving at Mr. Torkelson as he strode ankle-deep through
the muck toward his freight office. Twin Pines was a grubby
little town, but . . . it was starting to feel like home.

Emma watched the blacksmith and the farmer hoist
the heavy, red-hot wheel rim from the fire pit and drop it
in place over the wooden wheel. The blacksmith doused it
with a bucket of cold water and, with a satisfying hiss and
sizzle, the rim shrank to make a tight fit around the wheel.

"Come on." Jeremy motioned to Emma. He borrowed
a hammer from the smith, then handed it to Emma and
placed the stone he'd given her on the ground.

"Like this?" Emma raised the hammer above her head.

Jeremy snatched it from her. "No! Let me." He gave
the stone a careful rap, and it cracked open. He handed
her the two halves. "See? It's a geode."

Emma caught her breath. The stone was hollow, its
interior lined with glittering crystals. She'd never seen
anything so magical. "Are they diamonds?"

Jeremy snorted again. "Naw. They're just quartz crystals.
But I thought you'd like it."

Emma touched the crystals. Who would have guessed?

"Yes, Jeremy." Emma grinned. "I like it very much."

1867

A Peek into the Past

Looking Back: 1867

The dress reform movement that inspired Emma's mother began in the 1820s—but 40 years later, a woman in trousers was still considered shocking.

In Emma's day, fashionable women wore long, full skirts with six or seven starched petticoats underneath. Altogether, a woman might wear 12 layers of fabric around her waist! A snug corset helped support the weight of all that material. Although elegant, such clothing was uncomfortable and sometimes impaired a woman's ability to move, breathe, and digest food.

An 1867 fashion plate from a popular magazine, Godey's Ladies' Book

Several people in the early 1800s designed healthier styles for women. These costumes all resembled the Reform Dress that Emma's mother wears—a knee-length skirt worn over trousers.

In 1851, leaders of the new movement for women's suffrage appeared in public wearing such an outfit—which they called the Freedom Dress. One suffragist wrote, "Women are in bondage. Their clothes are a great hindrance to making them independent." Some suffragists used the costume to symbolize their campaign for women's right to vote.

Women brave enough to wear the Reform Dress found it practical and comfortable. A farmwife who wore a Reform Dress while helping her husband clear timber wrote, "Clothe yourselves in freedom's dress, despite the scoffs and sneers of the public."

Like Emma, however, most people found the Reform Dress scandalous. Some accused reformers of acting "mannish." Others laughed at them or decided they had "loose morals."

Suffragists who wore the Reform Dress received so much scorn that most gave up the costume, fearing it would hurt their main goal of gaining women the right to vote.

Public ridicule did not kill the dress reform movement, though. Some women wore the Reform Dress as they worked in the privacy of their homes or farms. And a few—like Emma's mother—believed that

The Reform Dress proved practical for hard-working women like this Wisconsin farmwife.

women would never be accepted as men's equals as long as their clothing prevented them from working and moving freely. These women found the courage to continue wearing their trouser costumes in public.

But by the mid-1860s, the dress reform movement had started to decline. The Civil War and the difficulties of rebuilding the nation afterward overshadowed other issues such as women's rights. American women didn't gain the right to vote until 1920—and it wasn't truly acceptable for them to wear pants in public until the 1930s.

During the Civil War, however, many women became involved in new ventures. Thousands kept farms and businesses running while men fought in the war. Some northern women, like Emma's mother, gained self-confidence and business experience by volunteering with the U.S. Sanitary Commission. This national organization worked to ensure clean and healthy conditions in Union army camps. Volunteers collected tons of food and medical supplies and raised more than $30 million, mostly by holding "Sanitary Fairs." These grand bazaars featured donated items for sale, restaurants, art galleries, military exhibits, bands, and parades. The fairs drew huge crowds and made up to $1 million.

When the war ended, many women were content to return to their former roles as wives and mothers. But others, like

HELP FOR **THE WOUNDED SOLDIERS**

The recent Terrible Battles in Tennessee, and the Great Struggle in progress in Virginia, call loudly upon all good citizens to do their utmost for the Relief of the Brave and Heroic Soldiers now suffering for the cause of our Country. Contributions of Hospital Clothing and Stores, especially of Articles named in the annexed list, are earnestly requested at the Depository of the U. S. Sanitary Commission in this City.

No. 1235 Chestnut Street,

The Smallest Contribution will be thankfully received, and all will be made immediately available for the Relief of the Wounded. We appeal especially to the

LADIES OF PHILADELPHIA

For their Aid and Sympathy in this Noble Work.

CHARLES J. STILLE,
WILLIAM H. ASHURST,
THOMAS KIMBER, Jr.
Committee on the Depository U. S. San.

ARTICLES MOST

Woolen Shirts
Pocket Handke
Slippers. Hospi

GREAT CENTRAL FAIR.

GREAT CENTRAL FAIR.

GOOD FOR **ONE ADMISSION.**

NEW JERSEY.

MINOR'S TICKET.

Mrs. Henderson, enjoyed their jobs and didn't want to give them up. The sparsely settled western territories beckoned women and men eager for new opportunities.

At the time of Emma's story, miners had been prospecting in Colorado for almost a decade. New gold strikes still created excitement—such as the discovery of a few nuggets in a partially dug well in 1862—but the first frenzy of gold fever had passed. Many men still headed to Colorado, however, to look for gold or to work in established mines. Shopkeepers like Mr. Boggs, saloon owners like Blackjack, freighters like Mr. Torkelson, and other businesspeople all hoped to make their livings by providing services that miners needed. Meanwhile, families like Jeremy's traveled west looking for good farmland at affordable prices.

And wherever miners and farmers and businesses went, a newspaper editor was sure to follow. In 1867 one editor wrote, "American pioneers carry with them the press and the type, and wherever they pitch their tent, be it in the wilderness of the interior, among the snow-covered peaks of the Sierra or on the sunny sea beach of the Pacific, there too must the newspaper appear."

Newspapers did

In 1869, this Utah newspaper staff used a tent as their office.

Idealized maps attracted settlers to western towns.

more than publish the news. They gave a sense of stability to tiny communities struggling to get established. Promoters worked hard to "boom" their towns by sending guidebooks, picturesque maps, and carefully composed newspaper editions east to attract new settlers—just as Jeremy's father hopes to do. If a small town failed, as many did, people who had invested in land sometimes lost their life's savings. Unscrupulous speculators like Mr. Spaulding published wildly exaggerated claims about their towns, much to the dismay of the new settlers they attracted.

Most newspaper editors were men—but there were a few women, too. The earliest women editors usually learned the newspaper business from their husbands, as Mrs. Henderson did. Girls of Emma's age were sometimes hired as typesetters because their fingers were small and nimble enough to handle the tiny pieces of type.

Western newspaper editors experienced many of the problems Emma and her

Editor Abigail Scott Duniway started an Oregon newspaper in 1871.

A bustling Colorado print shop

mother face in the fictional
town of Twin Pines. They struggled to get newsprint and ink
and sometimes improvised with
makeshift materials. One mischief-maker stole an editor's
press lever, just as Mr. Spaulding does. And in a few cases,
readers who disagreed with what they read in a newspaper
physically attacked the editor. More than one newspaper
staff worked with rifles at the ready.

Despite such hardships, three Colorado women ran
newspapers in the 1870s. In 1880 Caroline Romney had a
press hauled to Durango, where she worked from a tent.

In the West, these women found freedoms they might
not have had back east, where there were more workers
than jobs. On isolated ranches and in tiny towns, women
like Mrs. Henderson, Tildy Pearce, and Miss Amaretta
helped create the new West. And like Emma, many of
them came to appreciate the choices that living on the
western frontier provided.

*A woman homesteader
proudly receiving the
deed to her land*

AUTHOR'S NOTE

Twin Pines is a fictional place, but it resembles a number of small towns that grew in the Colorado foothills. Visiting the Colorado History Museum, the Golden Pioneer Museum, or Clear Creek History Park in Golden can provide glimpses of this fascinating time. And a walk through one of the Open Space parks, such as the City of Boulder's Doudy Draw, or Jefferson County's Elk Meadow or White Ranch Park, makes it easier to imagine the landscape as it was in 1867.

Thanks are due to Joan Severa, Curator Emeritus, Wisconsin Historical Society, who introduced me to the Reform Dress many years ago; and to Tracy Honn, Director of Silver Buckle Press at the University of Wisconsin–Madison, for demonstrating how a Washington Hand Press works. I'm also indebted to many people who shared their knowledge of Colorado's colorful history with me, including Michelle Zupan, Curator of Golden Pioneer Museum; Jim Wenzel, Interpretive Manager of Clear Creek History Park; Al Mosch, co-owner of the Phoenix Mine; and the photoarchivists of the Western History Photography Collection, Denver Public Library.

And as always, I'm grateful for the support of my family, my writing group, and the wonderful team at Pleasant Company.

ABOUT THE AUTHOR

Kathleen Ernst is a writer and historian who spent twelve years working at a living-history museum called Old World Wisconsin. While working on one of its restored farms, she once got to wear a modern-day reproduction of a Reform Dress! She thinks one of the best things about writing historical fiction is traveling to great places, like the foothills of Colorado's Rocky Mountains, to do research.

Ms. Ernst's first book in the History Mysteries series, *Trouble at Fort La Pointe,* was nominated for the 2001 Edgar Allan Poe Award for Best Children's Mystery.

She has also written four historical novels about the Civil War: *Ghosts of Vicksburg, Retreat from Gettysburg, The Bravest Girl in Sharpsburg,* and *The Night Riders of Harpers Ferry.* Her nonfiction book, *Too Afraid to Cry: Maryland Civilians in the Antietam Campaign,* was named a Book-of-the-Month Club/History Book Club Alternate Selection.

Free catalogue!

Welcome to a world that's all yours—because it's filled with the things girls love! Beautiful dolls that capture your heart. Books that send your imagination soaring. And games and pastimes that make being a girl great!

For your free American Girl® catalogue, return this postcard, call 1-800-845-0005, or visit our Web site at americangirl.com.

Send me a catalogue:

_____ / __ / __
Girl's name   Birth date

_____
Address

_____
City   State   Zip

_____
E-mail

(_____)
Phone   ❏ Home ❏ Work

_____
Parent's signature   12583i

Send my friend a catalogue:

_____
Name

_____
Address

_____
City   State   Zip
                            12591i

Try it risk-free!

American Girl® magazine is especially for girls 8 and up. Send for your preview issue today! Mail this card to receive a risk-free preview issue and start your one-year subscription. For just $19.95, you'll receive 6 bimonthly issues in all! If you don't love it right away, just write "cancel" on the invoice and return it to us. The preview issue is yours to keep, free!

Send bill to: (please print)

_____
Adult's name

_____
Address

_____
City   State   Zip

_____
Adult's signature

Send magazine to: (please print)

_____ / __ / __
Girl's name   Birth date

_____
Address

_____
City   State   Zip

Guarantee: You may cancel at any time for a full refund. Allow 4–6 weeks for first issue. Non-U.S. subscriptions $24 U.S., prepaid only.
Copyright © 2001 Pleasant Company   K21L1

AmericanGirl ®

PO BOX 620497
MIDDLETON WI 53562-0497

BUSINESS REPLY MAIL

FIRST-CLASS MAIL   PERMIT NO. 190   BOONE IA

POSTAGE WILL BE PAID BY ADDRESSEE

AmericanGirl ®

PO BOX 37311
BOONE IA 50037-2311